Courage on the Line

Cynthia Bates

James Lorimer & Company Ltd., Publishers
Toronto, 1999

First publication in the United States, 1999

James Lorimer & Company Ltd. acknowledges the support of the Department of Canadian Heritage and the Ontario Arts Council in the development of writing and publishing in Canada. We acknowledge the support of the Canada Council for the Arts for our publishing program.

Cover illustration: Norm Lanting

Canadian Cataloguing in Publication Data

Bates, Cynthia, 1950 -
   Courage on the line

(Sports series)
ISBN 1-55028-649-8 (bound) ISBN 1-55028-648-X (pbk.)

I. Title. II. Series: Sports series (Toronto, Ont.).

PS8553.A8263C68 1999   jC813'.54   C99-930330-9
PZ7.B37Co 1999

James Lorimer & Company Ltd.,
Publishers
35 Britain Street
Toronto, Ontario M5A 1R7

Printed and bound in Canada.

Distributed in the United States by:
Orca Book Publishers
P.O. Box 468
Custer, Washington
98240–0468

Contents

Prologue: The Nightmare   1

1   A New Beginning   3

2   Remembering   8

3   Fitting In   11

4   Party Time!   17

5   A Friendship Grows   25

6   More to Worry About   34

7   Things Could Be Better   39

8   The Tournament   45

9   A Reunion   53

10   The Aftermath   60

11   Amelie Tells All   67

12   Life Goes On   74

13   Basketball Camp   81

14   Getting Ready   87

15   The Championships   95

16   On the Line   104

Epilogue: The Courage to Forgive   116

To my children, Joe and Tia,
for limitless love and encouragement,
and for Little Cindi, Justice and Will.

Prologue

The Nightmare

Amelie struggled to awaken herself from one of the night-mares that had been tormenting her on and off for weeks. Her eyes finally opened and she looked with relief around her familiar room, which was bathed in the soft light of the full moon coming in through the window. She was damp with perspiration as if she had *really* been running rather than just dreaming about it.

Amelie sat up, tossed her warm quilt aside and swung her feet to the floor, feeling the thick softness of the carpet under her toes. She snapped on the bedside lamp and shook her head to try and clear it. Gazing around, she began to feel calmer. Over the holidays, which were now coming to an end, her mother had helped redecorate her bedroom, and Amelie had selected sunny yellow for the walls.

"Now it's the only room in the house that's not some shade of green," Amelie had teased her mother, who adored the colour.

They had then spent hours painting Amelie's dark furniture a glossy white. Amelie felt that the room reflected her personality better now.

My former personality, that is, she thought wistfully. She realized that it had been a while since any of her family or friends had teased her about her perpetually sunny disposition.

She stood up and looked at her reflection in the dresser mirror. There were shadows under her eyes that had become increasingly darker during the disastrous fall of her grade seven year at Queen Victoria Junior High.

She ran her fingers through the curly brown hair that framed her pale, lightly freckled face. Blowing a wayward lock from her forehead as she gazed into the mirror, Amelie was startled by the bleak look on her face.

"Come on, Amelie Louise Blair," she said to herself. "Lighten up!" Attempting a little smile, she managed only a forced and somewhat lopsided grin.

Pathetic, Amelie thought miserably. That about sums me up these days.

The nightmares had begun after the cross-country meet in late October. Amelie remembered how she had thought things couldn't get any worse, but this particular nightmare was even more unpleasant than the real thing.

In the nightmare, Amelie had finished first and won the gold medal, just as she had at the real event. But, in this dream version, hundreds of students in the stands were on their feet, pointing and calling out, "CHEATER!" as the medal was presented to her. She had jumped down from the podium and run from the stadium, but could not escape the taunts that followed on her heels. And above the roar, she heard Jessie's voice leading the chorus of jeers.

1

A New Beginning

Amelie was relieved. The holidays were over and she had finished the first week at her new school. No catastrophes had befallen her. Nellie McClung Middle School seemed okay. She liked most of her teachers and the students had been friendly enough. There were two girls in her class who had been particularly kind and had invited her to have lunch with them, so at least she didn't have to sit and eat her sandwich alone. It was strange to walk down the halls and not see familiar faces. But it was with a sense of relief that Amelie realized that she did not have to be *afraid* at school for the first time in two months.

Amelie had almost reached her locker in the first-floor hallway when she heard someone call her name. She turned around and saw her gym teacher, Ms. Bradford, approaching.

"I was just thinking about you, Amelie," the teacher greeted her pleasantly. "So? How did you enjoy your first week at McClung?"

"Oh, it was fine, Ms. Bradford," Amelie replied with a tentative smile. She wondered how much her teachers had been told about her transfer from Queen Victoria. "I mean, I guess it will take awhile for me to feel *really* comfortable ..."

"And that's just what I was thinking about!" Ms. Bradford interrupted. "I ran into your volleyball coach from Queen Vic at a meeting yesterday and she was saying how lucky we were to get you and how sorry she had been to see you leave. She had high praise for your game and, after seeing you in gym class this week, I'd have to agree with her."

And what else did she tell you, Amelie wondered, feeling herself blush from the compliment. "She was a good coach. I learned a lot from her," she finally replied. "But, mainly, I just love the game. I'll miss playing," she added wistfully.

"Our grade-seven team has a practice now. Why don't you come?" Ms. Bradford urged. "I can't put you on the team officially, but you could be a spare since there's usually at least one player absent. That way you could keep playing and working on your skills, and you'd be helping us out. What do you think?"

"Come to a practice now?" Amelie repeated dumbly. "I don't know." Was Ms. Bradford making this offer because she knew what had happened and felt sorry for her, Amelie wondered. She certainly didn't want anyone's pity. "My mom expects me to go straight home from school."

"You could call her," Ms. Bradford persisted. When Amelie didn't respond, she continued, "Listen, it would be a good way for you to get to know some of the girls who play sports at McClung. They're a great bunch!"

Now Amelie was sure Ms. Bradford was aware of her troubles at her former school, but she was reluctant to turn down this opportunity. "Well, okay, I can try my mom at work," she finally murmured.

"Great! Use the phone in my office." Ms. Bradford was already directing her down the hall. "If it's okay with your mom, grab your gym clothes and get changed. Just come to the gym when you're ready and I'll introduce you. You may already know some of the girls."

On the phone, Amelie found that her mother's enthusiasm was even greater than Ms. Bradford's. "That's perfect, honey," she responded after hearing Amelie's request to stay.

"If you're finishing at five, I can swing by after I close the gallery and pick you up, how's that?"

Amelie thanked her mother and hung up the phone, looking around Ms. Bradford's disheveled office with curiosity. How did the woman work in this chaos, she wondered. Ms. Bradford seemed so organized and in control; it was funny to Amelie to see this side of her.

After retrieving shorts and a T-shirt from her locker and quickly changing, Amelie made her way cautiously to the gym doors and peeked in through the long, rectangular window. The team was sitting on the floor facing Ms. Bradford, who was leaning toward them from the bench. Amelie felt a momentary surge of horror that not only did Ms. Bradford know about her past life at Queen Vic, but she was now telling the entire volleyball team!

Don't be ridiculous, she reasoned with herself. Even if the coach knew, there was no way she would share that story with her students!

Amelie took a deep breath and pulled the door open. She saw all heads turn at once in her direction and she was seized with the urge to turn and run. But then she noticed that most of the faces were smiling. At least no one looked hostile.

Ms. Bradford stood up and waved her over. "Girls," she was saying, "this is Amelie Blair, who has transferred recently from Queen Victoria."

"Emily?" one of the girls asked.

"Close," Ms. Bradford corrected. "It's 'a' like in 'at.' Amelie."

With everyone's head turned away from her, Ms. Bradford continued with a quick wink in Amelie's direction. "Amelie found out that the sports program at McClung is so much better than the one at Queen Vic, she begged her parents to let her transfer and they finally gave in."

The girls on the team laughed appreciatively at the light-hearted claim made by their coach. Amelie had learned that pride in its sports program was a deeply entrenched McClung tradition and she'd seen the school's display cases filled with trophies, medals and plaques.

Ms. Bradford introduced each of the girls while Amelie concentrated on trying to remember as many names as possible. The last two were the co-captains. Daphne Jones was short with fiery red hair and flashing green eyes. She shot Amelie a dazzling smile, revealing a mouthful of braces. The coach asked the other co-captain, Quyen Ha, to partner with Amelie for the warm-up drills.

Amelie found it hard not to stare at Quyen, who had offered Amelie a small but friendly smile during the introductions. She was, quite simply, the most beautiful girl Amelie had ever seen. Her skin was pale and flawless, her brown eyes were rounded almonds. Every feature was perfectly proportioned and placed on her heart-shaped face. Her shoulder-length, jet black hair, which she tied back as they started to practice, was cut in a straight line and she wore long bangs brushed off to the side. She was almost the same height as Amelie who, glancing around, discovered she was one of the tallest girls in the gym. Quyen was very slender but Amelie sensed power in the way she moved confidently to the ball.

Amelie and Quyen worked well together, talking little and matching each other skill for skill. When the team began spiking drills, Amelie and Quyen converted sets into attacks that had teammates ducking their heads if they happened to find themselves on the wrong side of the net.

"Nice hit, Amelie!" called Daphne, who seemed to be the team's strongest setter.

"Thanks for a great set!" replied Amelie over her shoulder as she went to retrieve the ball.

Before she knew it, the practice had ended and Ms. Bradford ran a quick cool-down, then called the team into a huddle for a closing cheer.

"Next practice, Monday at three-thirty. The McClung tournament is three weeks from today so I don't want anyone missing practices," Ms. Bradford announced firmly. "Unless, of course, you're on your deathbed," she added with a wink before turning away from the group. "One — two — three ..."

"COUGARS!" the girls all shouted together while Amelie pulled a sweatshirt over her damp T-shirt. She wasn't sure whether she should be participating in this part of the practice. Was she on the team or not?

"Hey, Amelie, what are you doing? Get over here!" called Daphne. "Come on, girls, let's do this again," she instructed, pulling Amelie into the huddle next to her. "Now don't forget which school you're at," Daphne whispered to her mischievously.

Amelie was pretty sure now that she wouldn't.

2

Remembering

Amelie spent most of the weekend trying to catch up in some of her subjects. Although she had all the same classes at McClung that she'd been taking at Queen Victoria, different material was being covered in science and math, and she'd come in the middle of unfamiliar units. School was challenging enough when she was up-to-speed, but feeling completely lost in at least two subjects was not Amelie's idea of a comfortable position to be in. Her mother had offered to hire a tutor but Amelie was holding off on that, knowing they couldn't afford it.

On Sunday afternoon, her father came into the kitchen where Amelie was studying. "You've been at the books all weekend, Sport. How about a break? We can just catch the half-price matinee," he said.

"That sounds like fun, Dad." Amelie flipped her science book closed and stood up to stretch. Her father was dressed to go, so she quickly slipped into her cozy, down jacket and pulled on her soft fleece hat and mitts. After stepping into her boots, Amelie stretched up to kiss her father on the cheek. They got into his ancient and dilapidated Land Rover, which he'd already started and left running to build up what little warmth the faulty heater could produce.

Amelie looked sideways at her father. "How are *you*, Daddy?" she asked, willing her eyes not to fill with tears. The arguments between her parents that Amelie had first noticed after returning from her grandparents' farm in Prince Edward Island the previous August had gradually increased. Amelie figured that this excursion to the movies was as much a chance for her father to get a break as it was to give her one.

Not that she blamed her mother. Amelie knew how her mother worried about money, and her dad had not yet been able to find another job since being laid off last summer. Still, her father was sensitive and Amelie believed that he was suffering under the pressure to find work, despite his attempts at cheerfulness.

Her father turned toward Amelie, his face serious. "I'm fine, Ammi, just fine. But I won't be so fine if I think you're worrying about me all the time." When Amelie didn't respond, he continued. "Your mother and I know it hasn't been easy for you and your brother lately. But you and Luke will have to trust that we're working things out as best we can. You do know that, don't you?" he asked hopefully.

Amelie collected her thoughts. "I guess," she said slowly, "but I hate all the arguing!"

"I know, Amelie. Just try to be understanding for now," her father responded. As if to close the matter, he put the car in reverse and pulled out of the driveway.

After a few minutes of silence, Amelie's father took a deep breath and asked, "So? How's the new school? Do you think things will be better there?"

"It's okay so far. I've got some extra work to do to catch up, but I'll manage." She paused and then added with a smile, "The volleyball coach invited me to come out and practise with the team. I'm only a spare player but at least I get to play a little in the practices."

Her father looked at Amelie fondly as they waited at a light. "That's wonderful, Ammi! I'll bet you won't be a spare for long, once they see how good you are."

"Oh, Daddy!"

They found a parking space on the same block as the Capital Place Theatre and Amelie's father turned off the engine.

"What about the girls?" he asked hesitantly. "Do they seem nice?"

"Yeah, they were very friendly to me. It was a weird feeling after … after everything at Queen Vic." Amelie opened her door, climbed out and waited for her father on the sidewalk.

A bitter January wind howled down the streets between the high-rise office buildings in downtown Ottawa, and they had to lean into it to make progress up the block. There was no chance to discuss the matter further.

Amelie found seats while her father went to buy popcorn and drinks. By the time he joined her, the theatre had darkened and the screen was starting to display scenes from coming attractions. The last part of the conversation with her father had dredged up memories of Jessie Tremaine, Amelie's best friend from the time they had started school, and Anna Archer, a girl who had turned Amelie's world upside down.

Amelie let her thoughts drift to the first day of grade seven at Queen Victoria, a time when she was still happy and looking forward to the year ahead.

Suddenly Amelie's father was nudging her with his elbow. "Earth to Amelie," he said. It was his favourite line whenever he caught her day-dreaming.

"What? Sorry, Daddy, I … I was just thinking about something."

She settled down in her seat, promising herself to try and keep her thoughts in the present from now on. Although, thanks to the nightmares, she suspected that it might be a hard promise to keep.

3

Fitting In

On Monday the two girls Amelie usually ate with were at a meeting and choir practice. When she entered the lunchroom, she made her way cautiously over to where Daphne sat with Quyen and other members of the volleyball team.

What if they don't want me to sit with them, she wondered, feeling insecure.

"Hi, Amelie!" several girls greeted her.

Daphne moved over to make room between herself and Quyen.

"How's it going, Amelie?" Quyen asked quietly.

Before she could answer, Daphne piped up, "What do you like to be called, anyway? Amelie? Amy? Mellie?"

"Most of my ..." Amelie began, then stopped short at the word *friends*. "Most people call me Ammi."

"Ammi. I like it," Daphne said with a nod.

"Thanks."

"House league games start in five minutes," a teammate named Jill announced. "We'd better get moving. Does your team play today, Quyen?"

"No, I'm reffing," Quyen answered, then turned to Amelie. "Why don't you come along, Ammi? Ms. Bradford is always looking for girls to help with reffing and score-keeping."

"Sounds like fun," Amelie replied. She was happy to be included, especially when it involved being in a gym.

Quickly finishing their lunches, most of the girls at the table rose together and headed out of the lunchroom and down the hall to the change room. Amelie felt a little like a tagalong but it was better than finding an isolated spot in one of the hallways to study, as she had been doing before.

The gym was packed with girls, sitting along both side walls. Two teams were on the court playing a game that, according to the 12-11 score, was quite exciting. The expressions on the players' faces varied from intensely involved to terrified that the ball might actually come to them and they would be expected to do something intelligent with it.

Amelie was enthralled with the energy level in the gym and everyone's involvement, either as a player, a spectator or an official. The noise level was deafening, especially when one of the teams scored and players and fans joined in boisterous cheering and clapping. Amelie spotted Ms. Bradford sitting next to the scoring table, seemingly as involved in the game as her young charges. As soon as the fifteenth point was scored by one of the teams, she jumped up from her bench and started to organize the next game.

"Quyen, you're reffing?" Ms. Bradford called over to where the girls were standing by the door. "Hey, Amelie, how about keeping score for this game?" she added.

"Sure." Amelie knew that there was no way her voice would carry over the din, so she nodded her agreement.

The rest of the lunch hour flew by and Amelie was sorry when the game she was scoring ended, followed closely by the first bell signaling the start of afternoon classes.

"Refereeing looks like so much fun!" Amelie grinned with enthusiasm as Quyen climbed down from the stand. Quyen started loosening the ropes that held the volleyball net in place and Amelie helped her fold the net and haul it over to hooks on the wall.

"Oh, it is!" Quyen agreed, as she lifted a post from the sleeve in the floor. "One of the bonuses is that, if you ref while you're here, you get invited back to work at the McClung Invitational after you go to high school. And *that* you get paid for!"

Amelie thought she would enjoy learning how to referee too and was disappointed when Quyen told her that this was the final week of house league. "These are playoff games this week. Ms. Bradford keeps the last two weeks before the Invitational for team practices."

"You mean the team will practise everyday at lunch *and* after school?" Amelie asked, surprised and concerned about how she would keep up with her schoolwork at that pace.

"No," laughed Quyen as the two girls carried the posts into the equipment room. Amelie thought Quyen's laughter had a musical quality to it and realized that it was the first time she had even heard her laugh.

"McClung has three different girls' teams that all play in our tournament so we have to share practice time," Quyen explained as they left the equipment room and moved out of the gym.

"Three teams!" Amelie cried. "This school is really into volleyball!"

"No kidding. Hey, you'd better run," Quyen advised, glancing at the hall clock. "One minute to the second bell. See you at practice," she said with a wave as she hurried through the doors leading to the nearby stairs.

* * *

By the end of the afternoon, Amelie was beside herself with anticipation for the volleyball practice. She recognized the possibility of belonging that she hadn't felt for a long time and she wanted nothing more than for this feeling to continue. Amelie knew only too well how quickly and unexpectedly that sense of security could be threatened and destroyed.

Nevertheless, she already felt happier than she had in months, although, in all honesty, the situation at home *did* seem to be getting worse. Almost daily, Amelie overheard bickering between her parents. They no longer seemed able to keep their disagreements quiet, which never failed to set Amelie's nerves on edge. They often seemed more civil to one another in the mornings, however, and Amelie would feel her despair lift until the next argument flared.

At school, math was a disaster. A major test was coming up in two weeks and, despite all the extra time Amelie was putting into it at home, she just wasn't getting it.

Today, however, nothing could dampen her enthusiasm as she looked forward to playing volleyball and getting to know her new friends better. The practice was intense, with Coach Bradford making minute adjustments to player form and position.

"Amelie, straighten those arms to pass! You're contacting the ball too close to your hands." The coach wandered among the pairs of girls executing bumping drills, telling them to make this or that correction.

For the last thirty minutes of practice, Ms. Bradford set up two lines of players for a scrimmage game. Amelie sat next to the coach on the bench. Everyone was there for this practice, so she accepted her role as the spare player. Amelie was impressed with the quality of play by this all-grade-seven team. She thought they were almost as good as her former team, which was half made up of grade eights.

"That's it, Daphne. Way to move to the ball! Great hit, Tara! Good try on the block, Quyen. Next time, spread your fingers and angle them down a little more." Ms. Bradford called out instructions and encouragement constantly. Amelie would have to get used to that. Her former coach had been very quiet.

"Okay, Tara, take a break. Amelie, substitute for Tara in position one. You're serving," Ms. Bradford instructed.

Amelie jumped off the bench. All the girls on her side of the net hustled to the middle of the court to give her high-fives. She was pumped, but evidently not focused, as she sent a bullet of an overhand serve into the top of the net. Amelie couldn't believe her bad luck for she did not often miss serves. She hung her head but was encouraged when her teammates called out, "Good try, Ammi!" "Don't worry about it!" and "Okay, let's get it back."

The strong team spirit inspired Amelie and she vowed to try even harder. She stayed on the court for the remainder of the scrimmage as Ms. Bradford substituted players every five minutes.

When the practice ended Amelie did not hesitate to join the team for the closing cheer. Afterwards, Ms. Bradford took her aside.

"Amelie, you're a fine player and you've got great spirit and leadership on the court. I feel badly that you won't get to play in our tournament."

"That's okay, Coach, I understand. There's always next year," Amelie smiled.

"True," the coach responded thoughtfully. "But I'd like you to come to the tournament anyway, if you can. The girls will appreciate your support. And, it's a fun event. You'll enjoy it!"

"Okay, Coach," Amelie agreed. "Well, if that's all, my mom's probably waiting outside for me. I'd better go."

They said goodbye and Amelie went to join the other girls.

"Great practice, Ammi!" Daphne announced when Amelie entered the change room. "You can really pound that ball!"

"Thanks," Amelie grinned. "I just think of it as my brother's head when he hides the remote on me or hogs the phone or ... well, just about *any* thought of my brother can turn into a good spike!"

The girls laughed appreciatively and Amelie realized once again that she was feeling comfortable with this group. No, more than just comfortable. She felt accepted.

4

Party Time!

During the next two weeks, Amelie's social life continued to improve as she got to know her teammates better and, in return, they appreciated her cheerfulness and quirky sense of humour. Daphne proved to be the team clown and seemed to never be in a bad mood.

But it was Quyen whose friendship Amelie enjoyed most. Quyen was easily the best player on their volleyball team, but never once had Amelie seen the slightest indication of impatience from her toward weaker teammates. In her strong, quiet manner, Quyen encouraged the other girls without intimidating them or acting superior. She was invariably calm and unflappable, even during the tensest moments on the court. Amelie was not surprised to find out that Quyen had been the only grade seven ever to play on the McClung team in the provincial championships held in Toronto last November.

Ms. Bradford asked a team from Hopevale Junior High, McClung's closest rivals, to come and play an exhibition game on the Friday of the week before the McClung tournament. Earlier in the week, Daphne had invited Amelie, Quyen and two other teammates for a pizza and sleepover party after the game.

When game time arrived, Amelie couldn't believe her further good fortune. "You're going to play today, Amelie.

Sophia has a doctor's appointment," Coach Bradford announced in the pre-game huddle.

Amelie could only grin in response. Next to her, Quyen squeezed her arm in support.

"Okay, girls," the coach began her pep talk, "this is a grade-seven team, like you. Watching them warm up, it looks like they have some good skills and two or three strong athletes." She let that observation sink in, then continued, "The difference is going to be teamwork. Whichever team can put together their skills, their strengths and their ability to play as a team will win this game. Remember, it's best two out of three, but let's not give up the first one. Ready? One — two — three ..."

"COUGARS!" the team shouted in unison.

Amelie thought that the six girls playing in the first game were the all-round strongest players on the team, even though she wasn't among them. Daphne and Mei-lin were the setters, Quyen and Layla were the middle blockers and Daria and Jill were the power hitters, which was Amelie's usual position. The team was quiet to start and fell behind 0-3 within the first few minutes of the game. Ms. Bradford called a time-out.

"Time to settle down, girls," Ms. Bradford said calmly to the team. "I know you're nervous, but you've got to start talking it up out there. Quyen, Daphne, you're the captains. Take charge!"

As soon as they were back on the floor, Daphne started calling out words of support to her teammates and, before long, every player was yelling, "Let's go, Cougars!" and "Good try!" or "Nice hit!" Daria got into a serving streak that put the McClung team ahead 11-5, before the Hopevale coach called a time-out. The Cougars finally won 15-7. The teams switched benches and Coach Bradford sent out the remaining six players for the second game.

Amelie, who was fired up to play in a real game again, led the team with words of encouragement and solid play. But she got poor passes from a nervous setter and had few opportunities to spike the ball effectively. No one on the Cougar side of the net could put together more than two good serves in a row and the team was defeated 5-15.

For the third game, Ms. Bradford put Amelie on the floor in Jill's place with the girls from the first game. With Daphne setting for her, Amelie scored points on four successful spikes and the Cougars took an 8-0 lead on brilliant serving by Quyen. Ms. Bradford substituted the bench onto the court and the McClung team won the deciding game of the match 15-3.

The girls were ecstatic with their victory. They lined up to congratulate their opponents on a well-played game and the two teams passed by each other under the net to shake hands. Afterwards, Amelie looked around for Quyen and spotted her talking with one of the Hopevale players, so she followed the rest of her happy teammates to the change room.

The air was electric with the excitement of the victory. Even the girls who had not played particularly well in the second game were celebrating. After all, they *had* maintained the lead and contributed to the win in the final game.

"Hey, girls, let's make sure we play this well in our tournament next week," Daphne urged. "We'll *really* have a good reason to celebrate if we win gold medals!"

Amelie was almost ready to go when Quyen finally appeared. The girls gave her a spontaneous cheer in recognition of her serving in the third game and she smiled, although the attention clearly embarrassed her. Several girls were starting to leave and Amelie cheerfully held up her hand for high-fives as they went by her bench on the way out. Those remaining would be joining Amelie, Daphne and Quyen for the evening. They included Mei-lin, a small, nervous girl who looked like she was afraid of her own shadow. On the volleyball court, however, she was steady, determined and never intimidated by the opposition. She and Quyen had been friends since their days in day care.

The other person going to Daphne's party was Jill, a tall, pretty, blond-haired girl who had an entertaining, dramatic streak to her personality. As a player, Jill was inconsistent, at times spectacular, at other times, disastrous. Unfortunately, there didn't seem to be any way of predicting how she would play on any given day. Daria had also been invited but she came from a very strict family that did not approve of "frivolous" activities, and she often told her friends that she was lucky her father even let her play sports.

"I think it's the team that's lucky," Amelie had replied.

The girls left the school and headed through the underpass of the Queensway toward Heritage Park. Daphne told her that the two blocks of grass, gardens, trees and footpaths, now covered in snow and ice, were used for cross-country and track practices by McClung coaches and students. The downtown Ottawa school was surrounded by a sea of asphalt, concrete and car exhaust and the nearby park was like an oasis in an inner-city environmental wasteland.

Daphne's house backed onto Heritage Park and, as the girls approached, Amelie couldn't help but gape. Compared to her compact two-storey east-end home, this house was nothing less than a mansion. The outside was white stucco with black trim and shutters and, instead of shingles, the steep roof was covered in red tiles.

As they entered through the front door, a comfortable-looking woman who Amelie assumed was Daphne's mother, met them in the foyer with a smile and collected their coats, hats, mitts and scarves while exchanging familiar greetings with Quyen, Mei-lin and Jill.

"Thank you, Claire," Daphne spoke affectionately to the woman, and Amelie realized that she must be the family's housekeeper.

"Oh!" Daphne exclaimed. "I almost forgot. Claire, this is Ammi. She's new at school and she's on our volleyball team. Ammi, this is Claire. She looks after us."

"I'm pleased to meet you, Ammi," the woman responded formally, but with warmth.

"Hi," replied Amelie shyly.

Of course, Amelie thought to herself, if Daphne's dad is a cabinet minister — she'd learned that from Quyen — why wouldn't they have help in their home? Obviously they could afford it.

Amelie looked around and had to remind herself to close her mouth. The house looked like it belonged in a magazine, but it had a comfortable feeling about it as well. The walls were painted a soft ivory colour and were hung with a variety of art. The high ceilings were criss-crossed with dark wood beams and there was rich, polished woodwork everywhere. Deep-pile, oriental carpets in warm, vibrant colours covered the gleaming hardwood floors. The furnishings were tasteful and inviting.

"Daphne," Amelie said when she finally found her tongue. "This is the most beautiful house I have ever been in."

Daphne laughed. "Thanks, Ammi. I love this house. I've lived here all my life."

Daphne started leading her friends up a winding staircase but Amelie lagged behind, peering curiously at each work of art she passed. Her mother had always worked in galleries and, growing up, Amelie had enjoyed her exposure to the world of art.

"Claire!" Daphne yelled from overhead. Amelie looked up to see Daphne leaning over the railing above her. "Can I phone for the pizza now? We're starved!"

"I just did it, love," returned Claire in an equally loud voice, emerging from what appeared to be the kitchen. "Two extra large, one vegetarian, one double-cheese and pepperoni?"

"Perfect!" Daphne cheered. "Thanks! Hey, come on up, Ammi, we're going to surf the net."

Amelie bounded up the stairs two at a time and joined her friends in Daphne's vast bedroom. The girls were gathered around a computer screen where Mei-lin was scrolling through a menu. After half an hour of checking out the Internet, the girls switched to computer games until there was a soft rap on the door. Daphne jumped up to open it and Amelie heard Claire say the pizza had arrived.

The girls gathered in a huge dining room at a table that Amelie thought probably sat at least twenty people. She looked out the frosted bay window into a yard that was floodlit, the light reflecting off snowdrifts and icicles that hung from an aluminum awning. The yard was not big and Amelie could see that it was surrounded by a high cedar fence with a gate at the back.

"Daphne, does that gate lead into the park you were saying gets used by the school for running?" Amelie asked.

"Yup," Daphne replied, a string of mozzarella cheese at the corner of her mouth. "Heart Attack Park," she giggled.

"Is that what it's called?" Amelie asked, shocked.

Everyone laughed except Quyen who, smiling, responded, "Of course not, Ammi. It's Heritage Park. Kids call it Heart Attack Park because we have to run there for gym classes and most of us are not crazy about running."

"Students sometimes collapse after fitness runs, the ones who aren't in good shape," added Mei-lin quietly.

"Oh, I get it," Amelie said, laughing now herself.

"Seriously, though, you guys had better get used to the idea of running if you want to be on the team next year," Jill said ominously.

"Ooh, that's right. I'd forgotten about Ms. Bradford's little obsession," responded Daphne. "Anyway, what difference does it make to you, Jill? You ran cross-country this year."

"You'd better believe it! And I still have my little finish tag to prove it. Yup, sixty-fifth out of seventy-three runners. Can't do much better than that."

Her friends laughed, but Amelie looked perplexed. "What are you talking about?" she asked, looking around the table at each smiling face.

Daphne explained. "The grade-eight volleyball team — well, including Quyen, who qualified to go this year — plays in the Provincial Cup in Toronto every year in November. The school rents a bus and the boys' and girls' teams leave on a Friday morning and don't come back until Sunday night. They stay in a hotel with a pool and eat out and play tons of volleyball. Everyone has a blast!"

Amelie looked even more puzzled. "I don't get it. What does that have to do with cross-country?"

"Oh, yeah," Daphne giggled. "Well, Ms. Bradford is big on cross-country as fitness training for other sports. So she says if you want to make the volleyball team in grade eight, you have to go out for cross-country."

"She sticks to it, too," Mei-lin added. "The best player in grade eight this year refused to do the running and, guess what?"

"She didn't play?" Amelie ventured. Everyone nodded solemnly.

Quyen looked at Amelie thoughtfully. "I hear *you're* quite the runner, Ammi."

Amelie froze. How could Quyen know about her running? She had never once mentioned a word about running since she'd arrived at McClung. Where was Quyen going with this? Was it the cross-country fiasco she had somehow found out about? What else did she know? Did she intend to expose Amelie's past in front of her new friends? Panicky questions raced through her mind.

When Amelie did not respond, Quyen looked at her with genuine regret. "I'm sorry, Ammi, I should have known you wouldn't brag about yourself."

"What in the world are you talking about, Quyen?" Daphne demanded. "Brag about what?"

Amelie could only manage one word. "Brag?" she whispered.

Quyen looked stricken. Amelie almost felt sorry for *her*. She had never seen her new friend rattled.

"It's just that my friend from Chinese school, Bonnie Tam," Quyen began, then turned to Mei-lin. "You know Bonnie, Mei? She was on the Hopevale team we played this afternoon." Mei-lin nodded and Quyen continued, looking at Amelie. "Bonnie recognized you today and she was telling me what an incredible race you ran at the cross-country meet last fall."

Quyen looked around at the rest of the girls at the table. "Ammi won the gold medal."

"Cool!"

"Wow!"

"Awesome!"

Quyen's attention came back to Amelie. "I'm really sorry, Ammi, I should have talked to you privately first."

"No, no, it's okay, Quyen. No big deal," Amelie assured her, smiling weakly and at last able to exhale again. Inside, Amelie breathed a huge sigh of relief. She somehow felt like she had just managed to survive a social crisis for which she had been completely unprepared.

5

A Friendship Grows

After supper, the girls gathered in Daphne's family room to watch movies. By 11:00, some of them were yawning and Daphne led them back upstairs to her room where sleeping bags had been unrolled and pillows arranged on the thick, plush carpeting.

"Are your parents home, Daphne?" Amelie asked, returning from brushing her teeth in Daphne's own "en suite" bathroom. When she saw the solemn look on her friend's face and the discomfort of the other girls, she immediately regretted the question.

Then Daphne offered her a weak smile. "My dad's out of town. He'll be back sometime tomorrow. My mother ... I ... I don't have a mother. That's why we have Claire. She lives here and looks after us."

"Oh ..." Amelie let her response trail off. She had no idea what to say.

"Hey, did any of you notice Jason and the other guys from the boys' team at our game today?" Jill asked excitedly. Amelie could have hugged her for changing the subject.

"Other guys?" Daphne grinned, apparently recovered from the previous exchange. "You mean you noticed there was someone else there besides Jason?"

Jill turned red. "Of course. Everyone was there!"

Her friends laughed as they rearranged their sleeping bags and settled in. "Jill has a crush on the captain of the boys' team, Ammi. And I noticed he was cheering every good serve and spike she made this afternoon," Daphne said, winking at Amelie.

"Yeah, right, like I made *any*!" Jill cried indignantly. "I was terrible today," she added miserably.

"You were not," Quyen said softly but firmly. "At the next practice, I hope Coach B. works on serving. We could all use some extra practice."

Amelie flashed on Quyen serving six aces in a row in the third game. The run of hard serves hitting the floor at their feet had totally demoralized the Hopevale team and had set the final victory in motion.

And here she is, Amelie thought, trying to make Jill, who *had* served dreadfully, feel better by saying that we all need the practice. Amelie's admiration for Quyen continued to grow.

"Anyway, back to an *interesting* subject," Daphne quipped mischievously from her bed. "What do you think about the boys at McClung, Ammi? Are they cuter than Queen Vic guys?"

Amelie felt herself starting to blush and was glad that Daphne had turned out the lights. She hadn't really given boys a lot of thought. That kind of interest had been Jessie's department. She searched for a response that would not set her apart from her peers. The face of a long-time friend came to mind.

"Well," she began tentatively, "I did have a good friend at Queen Vic who was a guy and, um, he was ... that is, he *is* pretty cute," she finished lamely.

"Oh, don't mind Daphne, Ammi," Quyen said, zipping into a sleeping bag next to Amelie's. "Everyone knows she's boy-crazy," she added with an air of affectionate teasing.

"Look who's talking!" Daphne protested, laughing. "Was there one single guy you didn't dance with at the Christmas dance? Including most of the grade eights?"

"The difference is," Jill spoke up from across the room, "it's not Quyen who's boy-crazy." She paused. "It's the guys who are Quyen-crazy!"

Everyone laughed at that. "You're right," Daphne lamented. "That's the only reason I hang out with her — to get her leftovers!"

"Okay, okay, enough!" Quyen spoke up good-naturedly. "Get some rest. You sound like you're sleep deprived."

There were a few more halfhearted remarks about school, boys and volleyball, but gradually quiet descended on the room. Amelie lay awake and watched the moon that had risen outside Daphne's window. She listened to the sounds of deep, steady breathing, indicating that the others had drifted off to sleep.

This has been a great day, she thought to herself. But there had been moments of concern, panic even. The discussion about the cross-country meet came back to her again and she wondered how she could realistically keep what had happened at Queen Victoria a secret from her new friends. Just as Quyen had talked to Bonnie Tam, someone was bound to talk to someone who knew someone who ...

"Ammi? You asleep?" came a soft whisper from beside her.

"Quyen? No, I was just looking at the moon," Amelie answered in a low voice so as not to disturb the others.

"I ... I just want you to know how sorry I am about bringing up the cross-country thing at supper." Quyen spoke quietly but with urgency. "I should have ..."

"Forget it, Quyen," Amelie replied gently. "It really doesn't matter."

"Yes, it does." Quyen paused and Amelie waited for her to go on. "I *hate* it when people talk about *me* like that. It's almost like *they're* trying to take credit for something *I've* done. I really didn't mean to do that."

"Oh, Quyen, please, I didn't feel like that at all," Amelie insisted. "I was just surprised, that's all."

"Surprised?" Quyen questioned, still whispering softly. "You turned as white as a ghost. I was afraid you were going to faint! What was *that* about?"

Amelie didn't answer right away. She didn't trust her voice not to betray her.

Quyen responded to her silence. "You still awake?"

"Yeah," Amelie began. "Listen, Quyen, there's a long story behind it." She drew a deep breath. "But I'm not ready to tell it yet. I hope you can understand." She knew this was risky but her intuition told her that Quyen was the one person she could trust this far. Whether she could trust her all the way would remain to be seen.

Quyen did not respond immediately and Amelie wondered if she had misjudged her. "Ammi, whatever you want to tell, whenever you want to tell it, I'll be glad to listen," she finally said gently.

"Thanks, Quyen."

Several minutes passed.

"Ammi?" It was Quyen again.

"Yeah?"

"About Daphne's mom …"

"Uh huh?"

"She left when Daphne was just a baby. It was a big scandal. Apparently she couldn't deal with political life, or something like that. Daph's pretty sensitive about it."

Amelie thought about that. She certainly could understand Daphne's sensitivity. After all, Amelie was sensitive about her parents and they were still together!

"Didn't she want to take Daphne with her?" Amelie asked.

"Daphne *never* talks about her mom. My parents told me that Daphne's mother tried to get custody after she left, but her dad was powerful, even back then. He not only got custody of Daphne, he had her mom declared an unfit parent, or something. Daphne hasn't seen her since she was two."

"That's really sad," Amelie whispered. "Thanks for filling me in, Quyen. I'll try not to put my foot in my mouth again."

"Don't worry about it. You didn't know."

It was true. There was so much she didn't know about all these new friends. Even Quyen, who had now seemed to indicate that she trusted Amelie. Quyen was the biggest mystery of all! She certainly commanded a great deal of respect from her peers. Amelie sensed from their earlier discussion that, for Quyen, certain topics about herself were "off limits" in casual conversation. Amelie remembered how Quyen had become even quieter than usual when Daphne had boasted to Amelie about how Quyen was in the school's gifted class. Daphne had changed the subject fast when she'd noticed how Quyen's face had darkened.

Before long, Quyen had fallen asleep. Amelie lay awake, thinking about Quyen's questions until her mind travelled back to memories of Anna Archer and the day of the cross-country meet.

* * *

From the time they had started school, Jessie Tremaine had been Amelie's best friend. They had played together as young children and then gradually developed a common interest in running and playing sports as they'd gotten older. Together, Amelie and Jessie had eagerly looked forward to attending Queen Victoria Junior High where they knew that the opportunities to play sports would be greater than at the tiny, neighbourhood elementary school they'd attended since kindergarten.

Then, something unexpected had happened. Amelie had arrived home last August from P.E.I. to find that Jessie had become close friends with Anna Archer, a rich, sophisticated girl she had met at summer camp, who would also be attending Queen Victoria. Over the summer, Jessie had gone from being Amelie's mischievous, pony-tailed pal to a boy-crazy stranger in make-up who seemed to have lost the enthusiasm for play that she and Amelie had shared for so many years.

Jessie hadn't exactly dropped Amelie's friendship, but Anna Archer seemed to resent Amelie. Under Anna's influence, the distance between Jessie and Amelie had gradually widened. Amelie grew increasingly uncomfortable in their company, especially when Anna started being openly mean to Amelie, making nasty remarks about her being a "goody two shoes" and a "teacher's pet." She always made her comments with a little smile so that it sounded like she was only teasing. Jessie would laugh along with Anna as if it were all in good fun, but Amelie sensed Anna's real dislike. To make matters worse, Jessie would not listen to any criticism of her new friend. She was like a puppy tagging along happily after its master.

Jessie and Anna participated in sports, but with less dedication than Amelie. That, too, became an issue that Anna used against Amelie, saying that she was a "showoff" and a "gloryseeker."

The cross-country meet had been Amelie's first major wound.

By the time the meet rolled around, Anna had almost succeeded in alienating Amelie not only from Jessie, but from the rest of their group as well. Amelie, naive and trusting, could not figure out how everything had gone so terribly wrong.

To make matters worse, Amelie was competing against Anna at the district cross-country championships. Jessie had injured herself training during the previous week and would have to watch the races from the stands.

When their race began, Amelie avoided taking an early lead, which she could have easily done, on the other seventy-six runners. She remained in the middle of the pack with Anna in her sights for the first kilometre. Having trained together as part of the Queen Victoria team, Amelie knew that Anna was an excellent runner, but she also remembered how Anna slacked off in practice. Amelie didn't think she could possibly be in top form for the challenging course ahead.

When she saw that Anna was starting to move up into the lead group, Amelie moved as well. Just past the halfway mark, she and Anna were running through an isolated section of the course that wound for 500 metres through a thick stand of trees above, but parallel to the path leading to the final approach. Normally, there was a coach supervising at this point because it was easy for a runner to cut more than half a kilometre from the course.

The girls were both running hard now. The lead pack of four runners had already cleared the trees and was now into the first loop of the final kilometre.

"How are you doing, Anna?" Ammi ventured from behind. She hadn't totally given up trying to be friendly.

Anna looked over her shoulder and slowed down. "How do you think?" she asked bitterly. "I'm dead. I went out too fast, there's no way I can finish this thing."

Amelie pulled even with Anna and replied earnestly, "Sure you can. I'll run it in with you."

Anna looked angrily at Amelie. "I said I couldn't do it. Now, get going before everyone else catches up. I don't want you saying I kept you from winning this race."

"But, I would never ..." Amelie started, then realized it was pointless. She ran down the path, leaving Anna behind.

Amelie caught the lead runners as they were struggling up the final hill that marked the last 500 metres of the race. Only the first- and second-place runners appeared to have much energy left but Amelie flew by them like she had just begun. She entered the stadium alone and threw herself, physically and emotionally drained, across the finish line.

Exhausted, Amelie watched from the sidelines as Anna did complete the course after all. But she never noticed Anna speaking to meet officials and pointing a finger at her. Only later did she learn that Anna had accused her of cutting through the trees to the lower path. Three of the girls Amelie had passed on the hill were only too happy to believe Anna's story, based on their observation that Amelie had gone by them with an unusual amount of energy for that point in the race. The fourth girl, a runner from Hopevale Junior High named Bonnie Tam, had refused to back such an accusation with no evidence to support it.

Fortunately, the coach assigned to the treed area, who also happened to be from Hopevale, had only stepped out of Ammi and Anna's sight momentarily. She had moved from her station area briefly to watch Bonnie running on the lower path. But the coach had returned to the upper path in time to see the end of the exchange between Amelie and Anna and to witness Amelie moving out of the woods, without any deviation, along the specified course.

Amelie never even knew about the accusation until the bus ride back to school. Despite the challenge to her story, Anna maintained to her teammates that Amelie had cheated. Even Jessie, who had not yet been blatantly mean to Amelie, now refused to meet her gaze. Seated alone on an otherwise crowded bus, Ammi removed the gold medal from around her neck and stared out the window as hot tears of humiliation splashed onto the hand clutching the costly prize.

* * *

Well, thought Amelie sleepily, so much for my promise not to think about the past.

As she at last began to drift off, it occurred to Amelie that, just maybe, facing her painful memories while awake would keep them from haunting her while asleep. She could only hope.

6

More to Worry About

The after-school practice on Monday was tough.

"What's with all the sprints?" Daphne, red-faced and winded, complained to Amelie as they finished the third set. "I'm going to be too tired to do anything else."

"Something the matter, Daphne?" Ms. Bradford asked casually.

"Uh … no, Coach, nothing," Daphne responded, managing one of her disarming smiles. "I was just wondering about a water break."

"Ah, good thinking, Captain." The twinkle in Ms. Bradford's eye told Amelie that the coach was trying not to laugh. "All right girls, two minutes, then back in here for stretching. Quyen, you lead."

The girls who had forgotten their water bottles rushed greedily to the only water fountain. Amelie and Quyen sat down together and took long pulls from their bottles.

"How's the math going, Ammi?" Quyen inquired casually.

"I think I'm finally starting to figure out fractions."

Quyen smiled. "I'm sure you will. Let me know if I can help. My class has already finished that unit."

"That would …"

"Let's get going, girls!" Ms. Bradford ordered. "Daria, Daphne, Quyen. You're the receiving team. Everyone else is serving. I want to see three hits, girls. If you miss the serve-receive or send it back after only one contact, you join the serving line and the next three players take your place. Got it?"

Everyone hustled into position. The drill was quick paced and fun. The practice ended with a scrimmage and afterwards, at 5:45, thirteen exhausted, sweaty girls made their way to the change room and collapsed on the benches.

"What's she trying to do to us?" one girl asked the group in general.

"Toughen us up," replied Quyen simply.

Amelie added to the theory. "I think maybe Coach B. wants you to get a feel for what it might be like to play three matches in four hours on Friday. That's nine games! Could be pretty tiring."

"Yeah, you're right," Jill agreed. "I guess I didn't realize how important endurance is in this game."

Ms. Bradford entered the change room. "Sorry to intrude, girls. Tomorrow's practice at lunch will be a scrimmage against the grade eights." As she turned to leave, she added, "Bring your shirts."

"The grade eights?" Mei-lin said softly.

"Wow! That'll be so cool," Daphne crowed, showing more enthusiasm than she had any time during the past hour.

"Hmm …" Quyen reflected. "That should be interesting."

"Do you think we'll get humiliated?" Jill asked nobody in particular.

* * *

As it turned out, they didn't get humiliated. Beaten, but not humiliated. Ms. Bradford did not allow any spectators into the gym. They only had enough time for two games, which the girls all agreed was a good indication that they had played well.

"If we'd been terrible, the games would have been over in a flash," observed Jill as the girls reviewed the scrimmage after school over milk shakes at Ida's, a small restaurant across from the school, on the corner of Bank Street.

"Right," agreed Daphne. "And I think we served really well. For sure we scored some good points on them with Amelie's and Daria's spikes."

"You were setting really well, Daph," Amelie added. "And some of those tips you made over the blocker completely fooled them, Quyen."

"I even managed to put in a few serves for a change," Jill offered shyly.

"You were awesome, Jilly! The best I've seen you play," Amelie said enthusiastically, putting an arm around Jill's shoulder and shaking her playfully. Jill lit up under the praise.

"At least Ms. Bradford said she was happy with how we played," Mei-lin reminded her teammates. "Do you think she was pleased with her eights?"

"They were pretty good if you ask me!" Daphne responded.

"Well, I've got to run," Amelie announced, looking at her watch with regret. "Dad's picking me up at four-thirty so I can spend the next twenty-four hours studying for that math test," she complained, rolling her eyes.

"Oh, that's right. Good luck tomorrow, Ammi," said Daphne.

"Just try to relax," Quyen urged. "You'll do great."

Amelie left the restaurant and looked across the street to where her parents usually parked to wait for her. There was no one there yet. On the days when she had no activities after school, she was allowed to take the city bus home. But when she had a practice or stayed for extra help, her parents insisted that she wait for one of them to pick her up because it grew dark so early. She couldn't wait until spring came and the days were longer. Then she could make her own way home every day and not cause her parents any worry.

As she waited for the familiar shape of the old Land Rover to appear at the school, Amelie was startled by a familiar honk and looked around to see her mother's car sitting in front of the Bank Street side of the restaurant. She smiled and ran over to the car, waving through the restaurant window at her friends, who were still gathered inside.

She opened the door and climbed into the car. "What's going on?" she asked cheerfully as she leaned over to kiss her mother's cheek. "You usually work Wednesday nights. I thought Dad was going to pick me up."

Amelie's smile faded as she watched her mother chew on her lower lip. "I didn't go to work today, Ammi," she finally responded.

Amelie felt her spirits plummeting. "What's the matter? Did something happen? Is Daddy ... or Luke ..."

"Oh no, Ammi, everyone is fine, that is ... well, no one is hurt ... exactly ..." Her mother's stumbling explanation as she pulled onto the Queensway ramp was doing nothing to ease Amelie's distress.

"Mom, tell me! What's going on? Where's Daddy?"

"Calm down, Amelie," her mother finally managed in a more reassuring tone. "Your father is fine. But I have, um, disappointing news for you." She paused. "Your dad moved out of the house today."

Amelie caught an anxious glance from her mother but remained silent.

"Ammi?" They had left the expressway and were approaching their east-end street.

"Where did he go?" Amelie asked softly. She felt that if she tried to say more, the sobs that were building up inside her chest would unleash a torrent of emotion that she might never get back under control.

Amelie's mother pulled into their driveway and parked the car. With both hands resting on top of the steering wheel, she hung her head. When she answered, her voice was a whisper. "He's gone to stay with Uncle Lou and Auntie Vi for now."

Amelie looked at her house. The driveway and front walk had been neatly shoveled and smoke rose from the chimney. A warm, yellow light shone softly from the living room window. She had lived in this house since kindergarten. They had just moved in when she first met Jessie. At the moment, it no longer seemed like home.

7

Things Could Be Better

Amelie was hurrying from her locker in an attempt to avoid having to go to the office for a late slip, when Ms. Bradford stepped out of her office and into Amelie's path.

Not now, Amelie thought desperately.

"We missed you at practice this morning, Ammi," Ms. Bradford said in a neutral voice.

"I'm so sorry, Ms. B.," Amelie apologized, not stopping in hopes of avoiding a long conversation. "I was up late studying for this big math test I have this morning and ... well ... I had a little trouble waking up." She was now backing up toward the double doors at the stairwell.

"Could you drop into the gym at lunch today? I have a practice with the eights but I need to talk to you about something."

Amelie was backed up against the doors now. "Yeah, sure, Ms. B. I'll be there. I gotta run now."

"Okay, Ammi. Good luck on your test," the teacher called as Amelie pushed through the doors.

Just what I need, Amelie fretted as she hurried up the stairs, something else to stress me out. I wonder what bad news Ms. Bradford has for me. Maybe she'll kick me off the team for missing that practice this morning. It's not like I'm contributing anything this weekend anyway ...

Amelie's thoughts drifted off as she tried to focus her mind on numbers: adding, subtracting, multiplying, dividing, reducing and converting fractions. The late bell sounded just as she crossed the threshold into her homeroom. She stood for "O Canada" and listened absently to the announcements until her attention was grabbed by one being made by the athletic association president.

"... Invitational begins tonight. If you signed up to keep score or work in the canteen, please be sure to show up for your shift. We need all the volunteers we can get to make this another awesome McClung tournament!"

"Tonight?" Amelie said aloud to herself. She thought the tournament started the next day. In fact she was certain that it was Friday her team was playing.

The bell sounded and Amelie gathered her books and rose with the class to head to double math and the dreaded fractions test. Out in the crowded hallway, she managed to catch up with one of the girls in her class who was on the team.

"Hey, Ammi, did you study for this?" her classmate asked without enthusiasm.

"A little." The standard response. "Listen," she continued as the two girls threaded their way through the corridor, "what did that announcement mean about the tournament being on tonight? I thought it started tomorrow."

"No, that's just our pool. The grade eights play tomorrow, too. But there are other pools playing tonight, like the one our "B" team is in. I'm going to stay and watch. You?"

"I wasn't planning to. I've got to go straight home today." They had arrived at the math classroom. "Good luck on the test," Amelie added as she went to her desk.

Amelie was relieved that she hadn't gotten her dates wrong. She was meeting her father and brother after school and they were going out for supper. *That* was something she wasn't going to miss for any reason!

The next hour and a half dragged by as Amelie struggled to concentrate on the numbers in front of her. Now what was the rule about dividing fractions, she agonized. Something about multiplying? Or was that reducing? Amelie became increasingly disheartened as she realized that all the time she had put into studying might as well have been spent sleeping. Everything was a jumble in her brain. She could barely remember how to find common denominators in order to add and subtract the simplest fractions. Everything beyond that basic task was a tangle of confusion. It was all she could do to keep from laying her head down the desk and having a good cry.

* * *

"What's with you, Ammi?" Daphne asked when the girls assembled in the lunchroom. "First you miss practice this morning. Now you look like you lost your best friend."

Amelie looked at Daphne sharply, then realized she was not being literal. "Sorry about the practice, Daph. I couldn't make it." As an afterthought, she added, " Ms. Bradford wants to see me. Any idea what that's about?"

"Not a clue. She didn't say anything to me."

"How did the math test go, Ammi?" Quyen inquired.

"Don't ask."

"That bad, eh?"

Amelie just rolled her eyes. "I'll see you guys," she said, picking up her lunch bag. "I'd better see what Coach B. wants."

Amelie tossed out her garbage as she left the lunchroom and headed across the hall to the gym.

"How was the math test?" Ms. Bradford asked as Amelie sat down on the bench next to her.

"Not so good," Amelie confessed. "I thought I was ready, but …"

"Well, maybe you did better than you think," Ms. Bradford said hopefully.

Amelie just shrugged. "I don't think so."

Ms. Bradford looked at her thoughtfully for a moment. "Anything else bugging you, Ammi? You seem distracted."

Amelie liked her teacher but at the moment she did not appreciate her nosing around in her business. "I'm a little tired, Ms. Bradford, that's all."

"Well, that's understandable. You've had to make a big adjustment, changing schools and everything."

Once again, Amelie found herself wondering just how much Ms. Bradford knew about her situation. It was definitely not something she was up to discussing now.

"Anyway," Ms. Bradford continued when Amelie didn't respond. "I was just wondering if you could help out at the tournament tonight. It looks like we might be short score-keepers."

"I'm sorry, Ms. Bradford, I have to go right home after school today," Amelie replied. "I just found out this morning that the tournament starts tonight!"

Ms. Bradford laughed. "Of course! I guess it didn't occur to me that you wouldn't be familiar with how our tournament works. But you must have known that your old team is sched-uled to play tonight?"

The statement, in the form of a question, hit Amelie like a slap in the face. "P … pardon me?" she stammered.

"The Queen Victoria team. They play tonight in the green pool. You didn't know?" Ms. Bradford was watching her closely now and Amelie realized that she must have looked as shocked as she felt.

"Queen Vic? Coming here?" she managed to ask. "No, I didn't know. The coach hadn't updated our schedule by the time I left."

Ms. Bradford frowned, then held up a finger as if suddenly remembering something. "Come to think of it, Queen Vic was a late entry. They took the place of a team that had to cancel." She looked closely at Amelie again. "Is something the matter, Amelie?"

Amelie felt a wave of panic rising up. Finally, she asked, "Are they in the same division as our team? "No," she said, answering her own question, "they must be in double "A," right?"

"Actually, it seems to me they *are* in our division. At least half the team is grade seven, isn't it?"

Amelie nodded.

"Yes, they would only have to go into double "A" if they had mostly grade eights. Nobody wants to play in the same division as our eights because their Provincial Cup experience makes them pretty tough to beat ..."

Ms. Bradford started going on and on about her grade-eight team and how great they were but Amelie was not paying any attention. All she could think of was that Jessie and Anna would be at McClung later that day. *At her school!* Where she thought she was safe.

"Ammi?"

Amelie snapped back to attention. "Sorry, Ms. Bradford. I was just thinking." She paused. "Will our team ever end up playing Queen Vic?"

"Possibly. It depends on how each team does in its preliminaries," she replied. "Why? You seem worried. Are they that good?" she asked with a smile.

"No, it's not that. It's just ..." Amelie didn't know how, didn't *want* to explain anything. It was too complicated, too painful, too everything.

Ms. Bradford stood to give some additional instruction to her team. While she was busy, Amelie took the opportunity to escape.

"Excuse me, Ms. Bradford, I've gotta go," Amelie murmured as she walked quickly toward the gym exit.

"See you tomorrow, Ammi," Ms. Bradford called to her.

As she headed for the washroom, Amelie thought back to Daphne's party. It had been less than a week ago and Amelie had felt hopeful, even happy. Now she felt like she was coming apart. First her parents. Then the math test. Now this. When would it end?

8

The Tournament

Supper with her father was an emotional event for Amelie. They had gone to Amelie's favourite Mexican restaurant, but the festive decor did not make up for the fact that Amelie was overwhelmed with sadness that her father no longer lived at home. Amelie's brother, Luke, was angry about the situation and sullenly ignored his father's attempts at conversation. Because she felt some sympathy for her dad, Amelie tried to make up for Luke's behaviour by chattering aimlessly about trivia, avoiding the topics that were really on her mind.

They were just finishing dessert when the inevitable question came from her father about how things were going at school. Amelie blinked at him, trying hard to hold back the tears that had gathered.

"I think, no, I *know* I'm failing math," she began, then grabbed a shuddering breath as the tears overflowed, and continued. "The Queen Vic team is playing in the McClung tournament at this very moment and *my* team might end up playing them on Saturday." Amelie finished by dropping her head into her hands and weeping softly. People around the unhappy threesome in the restaurant glanced curiously in their direction.

Luke glared at his father and finally spoke. "Are you happy?" he asked bitterly. "She's been going through all this crap and now she has to tell you about it in a restaurant because you're too selfish to stay at home with your family."

Their father responded softly. "Luke, you don't understand." He moved his chair closer to Amelie's and put an arm around her shoulder. "You two kids are more important to me than anything in the world."

"You could have fooled me," Luke replied evenly, standing up. Amelie looked at him, wiping her face with a serviette from the table. Luke returned her gaze. "Sorry, Ammi, I'm out of here. I'll catch a bus. See you at home."

While her father paid the bill, Amelie went to the restroom to wash her face. When she met him at the restaurant exit, her dad looked so sad she was afraid she might start crying all over again. He helped her into her jacket and Amelie waited as he put on his own coat, stepped into his heavy boots and secured a red, wool scarf around his neck and lower face.

Once they had made their way through the blowing snow and were settled into the Land Rover with a feeble wisp of heat tickling their faces, Peter Blair turned to Amelie and said, "I'm sorry you're still having problems with math, honey. It's not exactly *my* strength either, but you know I'll do my best to help you with it. You can call me at Uncle Lou's anytime and we'll arrange to get together." He headed out of the parking lot and down St. Laurent Boulevard toward Amelie's east end-home.

"Daddy," Amelie couldn't resist a weak laugh. "You helped me with my math last weekend and I *still* failed the test today!"

"Thanks, Ams," her father responded wryly, turning down her street.

"Just teasing, Daddy," Amelie said with an affectionate pat on his arm.

They pulled into the driveway.

"I know, Ammi," her father replied gently, putting the car into neutral and hesitating before turning to her and continuing. "It sounds like life is tough for you again right now. You sure as heck don't deserve all this."

"It's okay, Daddy. I'll manage."

"I know you will, Sport. I have faith in you. You're stronger than you give yourself credit for." He paused and opened his arms for a hug which Amelie happily returned. Then looking at her closely, he continued, "This thing with your mom and me, I know it's bad for you guys. It's rough for us too, but we've got some things to work through. You and Luke will have to be patient with us, Amelie."

"But do you still love her?" Amelie asked hopefully.

"I love my family with all my heart," Peter Blair responded without hesitation. "And that includes your mother."

"Good night, Daddy," Amelie said, planting a soft kiss on her father's cheek.

"See you soon, Sport," he smiled. "And good luck with the tournament. Everything will work out, you'll see."

Amelie slammed the car door and put her head down against the wind as she ran clumsily through the snow to the front porch of her house. Opening the door, she turned and waved to her father who was backing out of the driveway. Down the sidewalk, she saw the forlorn figure of her brother, bareheaded, hands stuffed into his coat pockets, approaching from the bus stop.

* * *

The next morning, after collecting books for morning classes from her locker, Amelie ducked across the hall into the lunchroom. This was where the tournament boards were posted that kept track of the games in each preliminary pool and provided the results needed to set up Saturday's playoff games.

"Great," Amelie whispered aloud to herself as she looked at the board for the green pool. Queen Victoria had finished first, defeating the Hopevale team Amelie and her friends had scrimmaged against the previous week, as well as two other schools. Hopevale, having finished second, would play the first-place team from the pool McClung was in. Queen Victoria would play the second-place team. Amelie closed her eyes and said a quick prayer that the Cougars would finish first. Or anything but second, she added silently, then immediately felt guilty.

Later that morning Amelie's math teacher paused long enough while returning her test to ask Amelie to stay behind after class for a moment. Although she had prepared herself for the worst, the 46 percent at the top of her paper was still disappointing and Amelie had to force herself to concentrate as her teacher took up the test with the class. It was little consolation to her when he announced that the overall results had not been great, with the class average being a mere 62 percent.

After class, Amelie was one of six students who had been asked to stay behind.

"I'll let you guys take a retest at the end of next week," the teacher explained. "But you'll have to attend remedial sessions with me between now and then."

Everyone, including Amelie, mumbled their acceptance and hurried out of the room to their next class.

Whew, thought Amelie, a second chance. She decided that she would take Quyen up on her offer to help her with math. Maybe she could come over on Sunday for a couple hours, Amelie thought as she went down the stairs on her way to family studies. We could study and maybe go tobogganing.

Amelie was starting to feel better as she entered the big classroom where rows of sewing machines occupied one side and four small kitchens, each decorated in a different colour scheme, made up the other. The aroma of freshly baked chocolate chip cookies, produced by the previous class, filled the air.

* * *

After school, the excitement in the change room was palpable as the McClung teams got into their uniforms and laced up their court shoes. Knee pads were pulled up and hair was tied back. Amelie went through the same preparations as her teammates although she would not be listed as a player on the score sheet.

In the gym, Amelie warmed up with Quyen since Jill was delayed by a class detention.

"Remember when you offered to help me with math the other day?" Amelie asked her partner as they practised their volleys at close range.

"Sure," Quyen responded, moving deftly to one side to retrieve an errant pass.

"Well …" Amelie paused before sharing her bad news. "I bombed the test, but there's a retest next Friday. Do you think you'd have time to come to my place on Sunday and go over a few things with me?" The girls had switched to short forearm passes, or "bumps."

"Sounds good," Quyen answered with a brief smile.

"Do you like tobogganing?" Amelie ventured, noticing Jill enter the gym. "We've got a great hill at the end of our street."

"I love it," Quyen replied. "This math help is sounding better and better," she added with an uncharacteristic grin.

"Great! You could stay for supper too if you want," Amelie offered spontaneously. "Well, I'd better sit down and let Jill warm up with you. Thanks, Quyen."

On her way over to the bench Amelie passed Jill with a high-five greeting. Ms. Bradford was filling in the team roster on the score sheet.

"Amelie, would you mind finishing this for me?" the coach requested. "I've got to sort out a referee scheduling problem in the other gym. I'll be right back."

Amelie took the clipboard and wrote the rest of her teammates' names on the sheet. She had to admit that she was a little disappointed that everyone had shown up, so there would be no chance that she would be called on to play.

The Cougars' first match was almost embarrassing — for their opponent. McClung won two games straight by scores of 15-0 and 15-2. The team scored most of its points on serves, so no one even got to break a sweat. The easy win did not dampen the enthusiasm of the players, but Ms. Bradford warned them not to become overconfident.

"That team was very inexperienced," their coach said seriously in their after-game meeting. "You will not have such an easy time with the next two teams, especially the one from Oshawa. You've got a two-game break so grab a bite to eat and come watch the eights play at five. Stay focused." She started to walk away, then turned back to the group, smiling. "That was some *great* serving, girls. Let's keep it up."

The girls hung around the lunchroom for a while, some snacking on junk food from the canteen, others virtuously gnawing on raw veggies brought from home. Daphne flitted about meeting and talking to girls from other teams along with McClung's male fans.

Amelie, Quyen, Mei-lin and Jill returned to the gym and squeezed together on the spectator benches to cheer on the McClung grade-eight team.

When the time came for them to play again, the Cougars found themselves in a much more competitive match than their previous one had been. They managed a win in the first game by a close score of 15-12. In the second, they trailed for most of the game. When they were down 6-13, Ms. Bradford called a time-out.

"Girls, let's turn this game around. We need some serving here. Quyen, you go in for Tara. Daria, you're in for Jill. Okay, let's go. One — two — three ..."

"COUGARS!" The girls in the huddle let out a big cheer and ran back onto the court. Ms. Bradford made her substitutions and the game was underway.

Once again Quyen came through and served seven straight points to even the score. Her next serve was successfully passed, set and spiked by the opposing team and Quyen's serve was lost. Fortunately, the opponent server fired the ball into the net. Daria then blistered two overhand aces to finish the game and match in favour of the Cougars.

Their last match, against the Oshawa Titans, was, as expected, the toughest one of the night. After winning a close first game, they fell in the second by a heartbreaking score of 15-17. Ms. Bradford made it clear before the third game that a win guaranteed them first place in the pool and a loss would mean second place. Amelie liked the way her coach spelled things out clearly to the team; Ms. Bradford was competitive but she was encouraging, too.

Amelie, sitting on the bench and watching her teammates take their positions, shuddered at the thought of having to play their semifinal against Queen Victoria the following day. She was ashamed to find herself already considering an excuse for missing tomorrow's tournament.

"Amelie!" Ms. Bradford was nudging her. "Are you daydreaming? You should be cheering the team! They need your support."

"Sorry, Coach," Amelie responded sheepishly. She looked at the scoreboard to find the teams tied at 3-3.

Giving her full attention now to the game, Amelie shouted her encouragement loudly and was thrilled as her teammates started to pull away from the Titans. "All right, Cougars!" she shouted.

She was also delighted to see that Jill was back on her game and scoring precious points both on serves and spikes. At last, game point was served by tiny Mei-lin and Amelie held her breath as the ball dropped to the floor in the middle of a triangle of Titan players, each of whom looked like she had expected one of the others to get it.

A roar went up in the gym as the McClung teammates converged in the middle of the court to hug and congratulate one another before shaking hands with the disappointed girls from Oshawa.

The next morning at 9:00, the Cougars would come up against Hopevale in a semifinal. Before that game, however, at 8:00, the Oshawa Titans would meet the Queen Victoria Royals in the other semifinal. The winners would play for gold medals at 11:00.

9

A Reunion

Amelie had set her alarm for 7:00, thinking that she just might work up the nerve to go to McClung early and peek through the doors at the first semifinal between her former friends and the Oshawa team. Instead, she ended up dragging her feet and arrived just fifteen minutes before her own team's match. Most of the girls were already on the floor warming up when Amelie entered the gym. Ms. Bradford motioned her over to the bench.

"Did you see Daria in the change room, Amelie?" the coach asked anxiously.

"No," Amelie replied. "She's not here?"

"Haven't seen her yet. And she's usually very reliable."

"Do you want me to try and phone her?" Amelie offered.

"Thanks, maybe I'd better do it," Ms. Bradford said, rising from the bench. She handed Amelie a small slip of paper. "Here's the line-up when the umpire is ready for it. Get them to huddle and do the cheer if I'm not back before the game starts."

After the coach had left, Amelie took the line-up to the scoring table and joined her teammates, who were now stretched out along the back line of the court, practising serves. Sixteen balls flew in every direction as the Hopevale team across the net were serving at the same time. She stood between Quyen and Daphne and waited for a ball to come her way.

"Must be nice to sleep in this morning," Daphne teased as she tapped a soft overhand floater toward the back line of the opponent's court.

"Hey, some people don't live five minutes from the school," Amelie responded, laughing. "Anyway, why do I need to be here early? I'm just the manager," she added with just a hint of sarcasm.

The referee blew a whistle signifying the end of the warm-up and both teams headed to their benches.

"Ms. Bradford went to find out what's up with Daria," Amelie explained. Then she announced the starting line-up. The team huddled, did the cheer and the first six players went to their positions on the floor. The Cougars had won the coin toss and had first serve. Mei-lin stood behind the serving line, focusing on the ball held aloft in her left hand and waiting for the referee's whistle.

McClung was up 2-0 when Ms. Bradford returned to the bench, looking somewhat agitated.

"Did you reach her, Coach?" Amelie inquired.

"Not Daria, I'm afraid. But I did have an interesting chat with her father," Ms. Bradford replied with a sigh.

Amelie didn't want to press her so she just waited to see if her coach would continue. On the court, the Cougars were playing steadily, managing to stay two or three points ahead of Hopevale.

Finally, Ms. Bradford explained. "Daria doesn't have per-mission to participate in school activities on Saturdays." When she saw Amelie's puzzled expression, Ms. Bradford added, "Poor thing, she must have been afraid to tell me."

"Daria? Afraid?"

"Well," Ms. Bradford replied, sighing again, "I guess I made it pretty clear that players were expected to make a commitment to the team and be available for all practices and games. Maybe Daria thought she could talk her father into letting her come, but ..." Ms. Bradford shrugged. "Unfortunately, we've already submitted our roster for this match and I can't substitute you in now."

"The team will be okay, Coach, you'll see. Look, we're up 12-7."

"Yeah, I'd better get in the game here," Ms. Bradford said, shaking her head as if to clear it. "Nice pass, Quyen!" she shouted. "Okay, Jill, this one's yours!"

It wasn't until after they had won the first game and were switching benches with the Hopevale team that Amelie noticed the familiar blue jerseys of the Queen Victoria team on the spectator benches. She spotted Jessie's blond head in the middle of the group but was surprised not to see Anna Archer sitting next to her. At that moment, Amelie was drawn into her team's huddle by Daphne.

"Okay, girls," Ms. Bradford was saying, "I would prefer to see us win this in two straight. That will give you more confidence going into the final and you won't be as tired. So just focus your energies and concentrate on every serve, every receive, every pass. Make intelligent choices. Let's go! One — two — three ..."

"COUGARS!" Once again the familiar rallying cry and six players took the floor.

Amelie noted that Quyen, Daphne and Mei-lin were back on the court for the second game. That meant Ms. Bradford was very serious about winning it. Amelie glanced back to the spectator section and caught Jessie looking at her intently. Amelie averted her eyes quickly and scanned the rest of the blue shirts for Anna. She spotted the tall, brown-haired girl standing at one of the entrances to the gym. Anna appeared to be deep in conversation with two boys from her school. Just then she looked up and locked eyes with Amelie. The look was one of pure contempt.

On the court, where Amelie had returned her attention, McClung was ahead by several points.

"Coach," Amelie said suddenly, "Who won the other semifinal?"

Ms. Bradford turned to her. "Oh, you didn't know? Your old team clobbered the Titans in two games straight. They're a pretty impressive-looking bunch. I don't think we would stand a chance against them if *you* were still on their team." She looked back to the court. "It's game point," she said excitedly. "Let's go, Daph!"

Amelie watched as Daphne served the ball deep into the Hopevale court. The receiving player swung at the ball hard enough to send it careening off the ceiling, ending the game and the match. Amelie experienced the opposing emotions of joy for her teammates and terror for herself as she joined the celebration at the back of the court and, feeling dazed, lined up to shake hands with the Hopevale players. The championship final would be played in an hour between McClung and Queen Victoria.

* * *

Amelie was feeling a little unsteady as the girls cleared the court to make room for a double "A" quarterfinal game. Ms. Bradford had told them to take five minutes for themselves then meet her in the lunchroom. Amelie broke away from her excited teammates and headed for the washroom.

"Hey, Ammi," she heard Quyen call from behind. "You okay?"

"Yeah, I'll be back in a minute," Amelie responded over her shoulder with as much assurance as she could. She did not want any company as she tried to sort through her confused feelings over being confronted with her former friends.

Amelie reached the washroom door and pushed her body against it in grateful anticipation of a moment's peace. To her horror, Anna Archer was standing at the mirror combing her long, shiny perfectly cut hair. She saw Amelie's reflection and turned toward her.

"So," Anna began as she faced Amelie, her voice dripping sarcasm, "look who's here. If it isn't the McClung Cougars' little mascot." She let the insult sink in for a brief moment as Amelie stood, frozen. "Not quite good enough to play? Too bad. What a shame. And you were such a *star* at Queen Vic."

Anna dropped her brush into her backpack and came toward Amelie, who still hadn't moved. As she came even with Amelie, Anna reached out her hand to grab the door handle and Amelie flinched. Anna laughed and paused with the door partway open, forcing Amelie back against the wall. "Guess you won't be winning any MVP awards today, huh?" And with that she breezed out, flicking the light switch as she went and leaving Amelie trembling in the cool, dark washroom.

The encounter brought back such a flood of nightmarish memories that Amelie thought she might faint. Just then the door started to swing toward her and she moved quickly out of the way to avoid getting hit. It was Quyen.

"Amelie!" she said when she saw her by the light from the hallway. "What's going on? What are you doing in here in the dark?" She switched on the light. "Hey, you look awful! What's the matter?"

"N ... nothing, Quyen, nothing at all," Amelie managed to stammer. "I was just feeling a little, I don't know, a little dizzy. I ... I didn't have any breakfast this morning."

"Well, let's go get you something to eat. Ms. Bradford sent me to find you. She's waiting for us before she starts the team meeting." Quyen took Amelie by the arm and led her out the door and down the hall.

As the two girls approached the lunchroom, Amelie saw that Ms. Bradford was standing alone in the hallway and was relieved that she would not have to make her explanations to the entire team. She felt pretty shaky.

"Ammi isn't feeling great, Coach," Quyen explained as she fished in her bag and pulled out an apple, which she handed to Amelie.

"What is it, Amelie? You seemed all right on the bench," Ms. Bradford enquired in a neutral voice.

"Just a little dizziness," Amelie mumbled.

"Well, let's hope it passes," Ms. Bradford responded. "I'm putting you in the line-up for the final. All the girls agree they want you to play," she added with a smile.

Amelie looked at her coach. She felt a sense of panic start to rise from the pit of her stomach.

"No," she whispered, then, "No," she said louder. "I can't. I'm sorry, I can't do it." Shaking her head, she started backing away from Quyen and Ms. Bradford, then turned and ran down the hall. Behind her, she heard Ms. Bradford say, "No, let her go."

Amelie stopped at her locker and ordered her trembling fingers to work the combination. When she got the lock off and the door open, she grabbed her jacket and bag, and, without bothering to close the locker, ran to the exit and out into the snow-covered school yard in her shorts and gym shoes. Slipping on her jacket and hooking the bag over one shoulder, Amelie crossed the street and made it to the stop just as a bus was approaching. She dragged herself up the steps, pulled her pass out of a jacket pocket and flashed it at the driver.

The bus was almost empty. Amelie went to the back and flopped down into a seat, dropping her bag on the floor. She swiped her hand in a circle over the window, clearing away some of the condensation. It didn't help her see through her own cloud of tears.

10

The Aftermath

Amelie arrived home to an empty house. Her mother wasn't expecting her until much later. Amelie had intended to stay at McClung until the tournament was over, regardless of how her team did, having offered to help with scorekeeping. She thought about calling her dad but decided she didn't really want to talk to anyone about what had happened.

I don't even know *myself* what happened, thought Amelie miserably. Was I crazy to get so upset about Anna's bullying?

The very thought of what her teammates and coach must think of her now was enough to make Amelie feel nauseous.

Sleep, she thought. I'll just go lay down for a little while.

Amelie climbed the stairs to her room, dragging her bag behind her by the strap. She couldn't believe she was so tired. It was only 11:00 in the morning. Laying down on her bed, still in her McClung uniform, Amelie closed her eyes and shut out the world. But as hard as she tried, she could not shut out the memories.

* * *

A week after the cross-country disaster, back in late October, Amelie had tried out for the Queen Victoria volleyball team. So had Jessie and Anna. They had been civil to her during the tryouts but definitely not friendly. On the final day, the coach had asked Amelie to stay behind after the practice had ended.

"You've got amazing skills for a grade seven student, Amelie," the coach began when the gym had cleared. "Did you play in elementary school?"

Amelie blushed with pleasure that the coach had noticed her out of all the girls trying out. "My school ran a house league but we didn't have school teams. I played quite a lot of beach volleyball last summer. You know, just fun games. Basketball is really my sport."

"Well, you're a fast learner, Amelie," the coach smiled.

"Thank you."

The coach continued, "I've heard rumours of some conflict between you and Jessie and Anna. Do you think you would be able to work together on a team?"

Amelie lowered her eyes to consider the question before responding. "Jessie and I have been friends since kindergarten. It's true that we've had problems lately, but I think we're getting over them now. I'm sure we'd make good teammates, Coach."

Amelie said good night to her coach and entered the change room, which had already cleared. She opened the locker where she had left her things and found a note stuck through one of the hooks. It read:

"If I don't make the team because you told the coach lies about me, you'd better watch out!"

Shaken, Amelie thought about going back into the gym to show the threatening note to the coach, but immediately thought better of it. The note was not signed but Amelie had no doubts about who had written it. She wondered briefly if Anna had done this on her own or if Jessie had gone along with it. Amelie changed quickly and left the building.

It was the end of a beautiful day, one of the last days of Indian summer, and the sun was still warm although it had already dropped to the horizon. It was going to be getting dark earlier and earlier, Amelie thought. And, despite the warmth of the late October afternoon, Amelie shivered.

* * *

"Amelie!" She could hear a familiar voice calling her name and she felt herself being pulled from the depths of sound sleep up through layers of unconsciousness and finally into wakefulness. For a moment, she was confused and couldn't figure out where she was and whether it was day or night. She looked at her bedside clock and saw that it was almost 4:00. The grey winter light coming through her curtains told her it was late afternoon.

"Amelie! Are you up there?" It was her mother calling from the bottom of the stairs.

"Yes, Mom," she replied and heard her mother start to mount the staircase. "I'm in my room. I was just having a little nap."

Her mother appeared in the doorway, looking puzzled. "I thought you were going to call me for a ride when the tournament was over. Were you sick?"

"No, Mom, I'm not sick," Amelie replied slowly. "But I almost was."

Marielle Blair entered her daughter's room and sat down on the end of the bed. "What do you mean, 'almost?'" she asked cautiously.

Amelie sighed. She knew she'd have to tell her mother eventually. She'd had to trust her parents with everything that had gone on at Queen Victoria. Otherwise she knew they would never have supported her moving to another school. Now it looked like she hadn't made a successful escape anyway.

It didn't take long to summarize the events of the morning, which already seemed like they had taken place days ago. To Amelie there was a dreamlike quality to the story as it unfolded, as if it related to someone else. It didn't seem possible that the situation that had severed her from old friendships and her former school had actually *followed* her to McClung.

Her mother listened without interruption, which surprised Amelie because of the way she had reacted a few months ago. "I'm going to sue that girl's parents!" she'd yelled. "She can't get away with harassing and bullying my daughter like that!" It had taken Amelie, Luke and their father hours to calm her down and get her to consider alternative action to pressing charges and suing. In the end, the family had all agreed that a change of school would be the best option for Amelie.

Now Marielle Blair sat with her lips pursed, considering the incident Amelie had just described. Finally she spoke, as if to herself, "What's the matter with her? What on earth did you ever do to deserve this treatment?" She looked at her daughter, perplexed. "Come on, Ammi, let's go put away the groceries and figure out what to have for supper. This situation is going to take some thought." Smiling, she reached out her hand to Amelie and pulled her up from the bed.

When they went into the kitchen, Amelie's mother pointed at the answering machine, which was flashing to indicate that there were messages waiting. "You didn't hear the phone? You must have *really* been unconscious." She hit the rewind button.

I wouldn't have answered even if I'd heard it, Amelie thought.

The first message was from Amelie's father, reminding her to call and let him know how the tournament had gone. The second was some girl calling for Luke. He got lots of those. The third was a friend of Marielle's, calling to suggest they go out for dinner one day next week.

Amelie froze when the next caller identified herself. "Hi, Ammi. It's Quyen. Why don't you pick up if you're there?" Pause. "Okay. Well, I'd like to talk. You know, maybe it'd be a good idea, so give me a call. I think you've got my number. Okay? I'll be home tonight."

The last message was from Quyen too. "Hey, Ammi, you home yet?" Pause. "Well, I thought you'd like to know that we won the championship. Yeah, I'll tell you all about it. It was kind of a weird match. Anyway, yeah, well, call me."

Just then, the phone rang. Amelie and her mother both jumped.

"I'm not here," Amelie whispered frantically to her mother, waving her arms for emphasis. "I'm not here," she repeated.

"Hello?" her mother spoke into the receiver, nodding her understanding at her daughter. "Ammi? No, I'm sorry, she's not available at the moment. Could I take a message?" She listened for a moment. "Quyen? You'd like her to call ... And she has your number ... What was the message again?" Pause. "Okay, thank you, Quyen, I'll see that Amelie gets it ... Yes, thank you again. Bye."

Marielle put down the phone and looked at Amelie. "Quyen wants you to call her. Of course you already knew that. She says that everything's 'cool,'" Marielle paused, holding up two fingers from each hand like quotation marks, "but she really wants to talk to you."

Amelie screwed up her face to give the impression that she was in complete agony. "I can't, Mom," she whined convincingly. "I just can't do it. What am I supposed to tell her? That everyone at my old school hated me and now they've come to McClung to torture me some more?"

"You tell her the truth, exactly what happened. Not that nonsense you're spouting now," Marielle replied calmly.

Amelie seemed to decide that it would be easier to relent a bit than to argue with her mother over the issue. "I'll phone her tomorrow." When she saw the doubtful look on her mother's face, she added, "I promise. I'll call her tomorrow."

Amelie and her mother spent a quiet evening in front of the television. Marielle had rented a movie that they'd been wanting to see. Luke had come in and had supper with them but went out with friends afterwards. He had been angry when he'd learned of the Anna Archer incident, but none of them could decide what, if anything, should be done about it. They all agreed that the worst part was the fact that Anna's behaviour had caused Amelie to abandon her team without explanation. And *that* was what had Amelie feeling so upset.

* * *

On Sunday, the family slept in while snow blew outside and settled in deep, soft drifts. After they'd finally got up and enjoyed a leisurely brunch, Amelie announced that she would be going to her room to study math.

Having taken the test and gone over her errors, Amelie saw that many of her mistakes had been careless ones. If she had checked her work more thoroughly before handing it in, she might have even passed. After an hour and a half of concentrated review, Amelie had just about had her fill of fractions. She looked out her bedroom window into the back yard and saw that the snow had finally stopped falling. The clouds were breaking up and the sun was starting to peek through.

"Amelie!" her mother called from the bottom of the stairs. "Could you come down here, please."

Nuts, thought Amelie, I'll bet she's going to start in about me calling Quyen. Amelie glanced at her clock. It was 1:30. Well, I guess I'd better get it over with, she decided, drawing a deep breath for courage.

She bounced down the stairs and entered the kitchen. Quyen was standing next to Amelie's mother, who was smiling as she took Quyen's coat and scarf. "Isn't this a nice surprise, Ammi?"

Quyen allowed herself a small smile. "You invited me over, remember? Math help? Tobogganing?"

Amelie was flabbergasted. Finally, she spoke. "Quyen! I ... I was just going to phone you. How did you get here?"

"My parents drove me. I got your address by matching your phone number to Peter Blair in the phone book. Pretty smart, eh?"

Amelie couldn't help but grin. It was so unlike Quyen to ever brag about anything she did.

"Why don't you and Quyen go upstairs where you can study in private. Or whatever," Marielle suggested.

11

Amelie Tells All

Amelie led Quyen up to her room and closed the door to ensure their privacy. She directed Quyen to a comfortable beanbag chair and sat down on the edge of her bed, picking nervously at a loose thread in the quilt.

"So?" Quyen began. "Don't you want to know about the finals yesterday?"

"Yeah," Amelie replied softly. "I do."

"Okay. Well, if you can believe it, we lost the first game."

"No!" Amelie was surprised. The Cougars never lost the first game of a match except when they'd played the grade eights.

"Yup. We stank," Quyen continued matter-of-factly. "We couldn't serve, we couldn't receive serve. We couldn't do anything. We lost 4-15."

"Oh my gosh, I can't even imagine that," Amelie responded.

"Well, imagine it. It happened. Ms. Bradford was in a state of shock. She hardly knew what to say to us in time-outs. No substitutions made any difference." Quyen appeared to be enjoying herself.

"So? You said you won the championship!" Amelie urged.

"We did. That old team of yours is something else. They've got a good setter, a short blond girl."

"Jessie," Amelie whispered.

"Yeah, I think that was her name. And they have this tall girl, she looks like a model. Great spiker."

Amelie felt Quyen's eyes on her.

"In fact," Quyen continued, "it seems to me that that's the girl who came out of the washroom yesterday just before I went in and found you in the dark."

"Yes." Amelie's voice had dropped so low it could hardly be heard.

"Ammi," Quyen said gently, "do you remember at Daph's party when you said there was something you weren't ready to talk about?"

Amelie nodded.

"Are you ready now?" Quyen asked.

Amelie nodded again and took a deep breath. "But first, I'd like to know what happened after I ran out of there like some kind of lunatic yesterday. Do you think I upset everything and that's why you lost the first game?"

"Nah," Quyen replied with a dismissive wave of her hand. "Ms. Bradford just told the team you'd gotten sick. For some reason, in that first game, we were intimidated and we let it get to us. But we clobbered them in the second and third games. You should have seen Jill. She didn't miss a thing. We all voted her our team MVP."

Amelie smiled. "Most Valuable Player. I'm so glad for Jilly. She must have been excited."

Quyen shook her head in wonder. "I've never seen her *that* excited." She rolled her eyes up toward the ceiling in contemplation. "Anyway, let's see. After you ran out, Ms. Bradford asked me if I knew anything about you being harassed by students from your old school. Of course I told her I didn't know anything and couldn't imagine why anyone would harass *you*!"

Amelie looked at Quyen. "It's a long story."

"I'm not in any rush."

Amelie started from the beginning, telling about how long she and Jessie had been friends and about all the things they had done together over the years, especially the sports activities. She explained about their training and their competitions and about how Jessie had always been the winner in sports and games but had been the follower in their friendship, cheerfully going along with Amelie's ideas and plans. When she got to the part where Anna Archer had entered the picture and Jessie was drifting away, Amelie had to slow down a little, dabbing at the corners of her eyes with tissues.

Quyen only interrupted to ask about things that weren't clear. When Amelie told the story of the cross-country meet, Quyen let out a little outraged gasp. "You've got to be kidding! She accused you of cheating even though there was a coach who saw the whole thing and said it wasn't true?"

"I don't think I'll ever understand that," Amelie replied thoughtfully.

"Okay, go on."

Amelie described the volleyball tryouts and the threatening note she'd received. She described how, when the team had been posted, someone had scrawled the word "LOSER" in big red letters next to her name.

"Then things got really bad," Amelie continued, gazing out her window at the snow, which had started falling again. "It's not like I didn't have any friends at all. I'd met lots of great people at school and one friend stuck by me through the whole thing. Only she moved to Vancouver over the holidays." She paused for a moment. "But, except for her, the girls I had always hung out with completely ..." Amelie's voice caught in her throat, "they completely rejected me," she finished in a whisper.

After a moment she began again. "All through November they, well, Anna especially, would make comments when I passed by in the hall. At volleyball, they went out of their way to avoid me. I think the coach started to figure out that something was messed up but she didn't know what to do.

"Anyway, at the beginning of December, we went to a tournament in Joliette, Quebec. Our coach's sister worked at the host school and invited our team. We did some fundraising and made arrangements to stay at the Château Joliette. It was a beautiful place. We were assigned three to a room. Jessie and Anna of course, and one of their friends, would room together and my friend and I and another one of Anna and Jessie's buddies would share another.

"At the last minute, my friend came down with the flu and couldn't go to the tournament. I thought about canceling too but, well, you know," Amelie shrugged. "I love to play. I didn't really think too much could happen." She shook her head.

"But you were wrong?" Quyen asked.

"Totally. Although the tournament itself was a lot of fun. We played well and went all the way to the final. We lost it to the host team but the match was good. In the closing ceremony, though, something terrible happened."

"What?" Quyen asked, looking dismayed.

Amelie grinned weakly. "I was presented with the tournament MVP medal."

"That's terrible?"

"It turned out to be. I don't know why I was selected, to tell you the truth. I played okay, but Jessie played better volleyball than anyone on our team. When she's at her best, she's as good a setter as Daph or Mei-lin."

"That's *your* opinion," Quyen teased. "Lucky for us, she wasn't that good yesterday."

"Anyway, our coach and her sister wanted the teams to go out for a nice dinner, you know, to celebrate. So we went back to the hotel and changed, then met in the dining room. The parent who had driven to the tournament was taking team pictures of us with our silver medals and the whole bit. Suddenly Anna Archer starts moaning and complaining that she doesn't feel well and pretty soon Jessie and the other two are saying that they have to go upstairs and lie down for awhile."

"Uh oh," Quyen interjected.

"Yeah, uh oh. The coach told the girls they could go up and rest and that she'd check on them in a little while. We went ahead and ordered our food and, just before it arrived, the coach went upstairs. When she came back to the dining room, she said all four girls were sound asleep and seemed to be fine so we carried on with supper. It was actually kind of nice for me to be with the grade eights, who had always been friendly to me.

"When we finished eating and picture taking and talking, everyone said good night and went upstairs. The rooms were spread out all over the hotel. I figured I'd be alone for the night because it seemed that my roommate was staying with her friends. When I opened the door to my room, I couldn't believe my eyes. My clothes had been taken out of my bag and scattered everywhere. The sheets and blankets had all been pulled off the beds and were thrown all over the place. Jessie, Anna and the other two were just sitting there enjoying my reaction. For the first time, I was scared."

"Why those little ..." Quyen's voice communicated her outrage at what she was hearing.

"Anna had my MVP medal and was swinging it around her finger. I was still standing near the door but it had closed behind me. It was like I couldn't move. Anna got up and walked over. She says, 'MVP, eh? Looks like that stands for Most Valueless Pig.' The others laughed but Anna was definitely the one in control. Then she says, 'Look at this pigsty. And your uniform, we found it in the toilet, you know. Did you put it in there to wash it out? How disgusting!'"

"She came closer to me and shoved me hard and I kind of stumbled backwards. Then she came toward me again and dangled the medal in front of my face and said, 'Jessie should have got this award. Anyone but you.' I was sure she was going to hit me then, but instead, she spit in my face. Then, suddenly, the door opened between me and her. It was our coach just standing there with her mouth hanging open, just missing Anna's spit."

Quyen's mouth, too, had been hanging open for the last part of Amelie's story, but all of a sudden she burst out laughing. Amelie looked at her like she was crazy then started giggling herself. "You should have seen our coach," Amelie said, now laughing harder. "All I could think was, wouldn't it have been something if she had stepped into the room one second earlier and Anna's spit *had* hit her in the face!" By now both girls were rolling on the floor, laughing hysterically.

When she'd recovered, Quyen said, "Hey, why don't we go tobogganing like we planned? You can tell me how it all ended on the way." Then she added, "Or, do you want to go over some math instead?"

"Are you kidding?" Amelie said, with a laugh. "I've been doing math since breakfast!"

The girls bundled up for their outing. Amelie didn't miss the look of relief on her mother's face when she told her what they were up to. They went out the kitchen door, picked up the long, old-fashioned wooden toboggan leaning against the house and started toward the park.

"Okay, don't keep me in suspense," Quyen said through the scarf that was wrapped around her face. "What happened?"

"Oh, about what you'd expect," Amelie replied. "Our coach had me move into the room she was sharing with the mother who had driven. After I packed my stuff, she made Anna and the others clean up the room. Then she rearranged all the room assignments, splitting the four girls and putting at least one grade eight with each one. The eights weren't too pleased."

"I don't blame them. Did they get punished at all when you got back to Ottawa?" Quyen asked as they arrived at the top of a hill that ran down through a long, shallow ravine behind a small townhouse development. "Ooh, this looks like fun."

"They were all suspended from school for five days. Our coach wanted them kicked off the team, too, but I heard that Anna's mother put some pressure on the principal and he said they could stay on the team. Mrs. Archer is on the school council."

Quyen made a noise to indicate her disgust.

"Yeah, our coach refused to keep working with the team so the principal made some new teacher take it over. The whole thing was nuts!"

"Wow, that's an amazing story! I am so happy that we beat them yesterday."

"Me, too, Quyen. Thanks."

"You know that girl? Anna?" Quyen said as the girls settled onto the toboggan. "She was red-carded in the third game. They threw her right out. She wouldn't even shake hands at the end. She was such a poor sport," she said as they pushed off and slid swiftly over the snow.

12

Life Goes On

Amelie returned to school on Monday with a renewed sense of hope. She was meeting Quyen early, before open basketball, so Quyen could support her when she went to see Ms. Bradford.

In her office, Ms. Bradford listened to an abbreviated version of the story Amelie had told Quyen and, at the end of it, admitted that she'd already heard a little bit through the gym teacher grapevine. "I appreciate your filling me in, Amelie," she said. "I certainly don't blame you for being scared. But, perhaps in the future, you could trust someone at McClung enough to let them know what's going on. You know the school *does* have policies in place to deal with bullying."

Quyen and Amelie looked at each other. Both knew that many students didn't expect to get much support from the school for this sort of thing. Most harassment was well hidden from the authorities.

"Yes, Ms. Bradford, I'll remember that," Amelie replied respectfully.

"Okay, let's get the gym open for b-ball. The Eastern Ontarios are just around the corner!"

"Aren't they, like, two months away, Coach?" Quyen asked, winking at Amelie as the girls trailed behind their teacher. Ms. Bradford had recently announced that McClung had been selected to host the Eastern Ontario Girls' Basketball Championships and the girls enjoyed teasing their teacher about the level of her enthusiasm.

"Two and a half actually, Quyen," Ms. Bradford responded lightly, "but we've got lots to do before then. Ah, Pauline ..."

"Good morning, Coach," greeted Pauline Duvall, stomping snow from her boots as she entered the lower hallway. "Hey, Quyen, Amelie, ready for some slam-dunk practice?"

"Maybe *we'll* get to where we can slam dunk, Pauline, but it'll never happen for you," Quyen teased her.

Pauline Duval had gone to McClung herself many years ago and was helping Ms. Bradford as a volunteer coach of the grade seven team while she worked on her master's degree at Ottawa University. She was very short for a basketball player, not even five foot one, but she had been recruited from her championship high-school team to play for York University, where she had been a star point guard for the past five years before returning home to Ottawa.

Amelie looked at Pauline's black hair, which was cut close to her scalp, and thought about what an easy style that must be for playing basketball. Better than this tangle of curls I've got to wrestle with, thought Amelie, imagining herself, none too attractively, with an almost-shaved head.

Pauline chuckled, a hearty, deep-throated laugh. Then her face became set in a serious, almost ferocious, expression that said, "Don't mess with me."

"Okay, smart-mouth," Pauline growled, responding to Quyen's earlier remark. "You want to start with a game of one-on-one or Horse? Doesn't matter to me. Name your game. You know I'm going to beat your butt regardless."

"One-on-one," Quyen responded grinning. "At least I can out rebound her," she whispered to Amelie.

"Don't count on it. I'll be in the gym in a minute." Pauline went into Ms. Bradford's office to change and Quyen and

Amelie went into the gym. It was still early and no other girls had arrived yet. Ms. Bradford was shooting lay-ups, first from one side, then the other.

"How about a game of twenty-one while I wait for Pauline?" asked Quyen.

"Hmm …" Amelie hesitated, then smiled. "Okay. I'm terrible at it though. Can't shoot free throws to save my life."

"Great, that'll boost my confidence for when I play Pauline," Quyen responded.

True to her word, Amelie lost a quick game to Quyen by a score of 3-21 as other girls started to fill the gym. When Pauline came in, it took her less than thirty seconds to score the two baskets necessary to win one-on-one against Quyen.

"You game?" Pauline asked, turning to Amelie, who had watched the quick defeat of her friend.

"Um … I …" Amelie stammered.

"Come on, let's do it!" Pauline laughed at Amelie's hesitation.

Pauline threw the ball in first to Amelie, who stood her ground long enough to bring Pauline out on defense. Amelie protected the ball in the triple-threat position her brother and father had drilled into her over the course of several summer sessions in the driveway.

Pauline was in the classic defensive position: feet wide apart, knees bent, both arms out to the sides, one of them stretched up to block a shot attempt. Amelie stepped onto her right foot in the direction most right-handed players would take to drive to the basket. As she'd hoped, Pauline shifted to cover her movement. In a flash, Amelie pivoted on her left foot, pulling the right one back across her body and sealing the space between Pauline and herself with the right side of her body. At the same time she took one dribble with her left hand, bringing her body around Pauline, picked up the ball, stepped left-right, and laid the ball up against the backboard off the fingertips of her left hand. The ball dropped through the net.

Amelie turned around to see Pauline standing where she'd left her with her hands on her hips, shaking her head and smiling. "My, my," she said, "I have *never* seen such a young girl make that move! Where did you learn to do that?"

Amelie took her place on the base line to throw the ball to Pauline. "Everyone in my family is a basketball fanatic. I've had lots of driveway coaching," Amelie replied proudly. She delivered a chest pass into Pauline's outstretched hands, then immediately moved to establish herself on defence. Before she could get within two steps of her opponent, Pauline had put up a perfect shot that arced gracefully into the air and swished through the net.

"One-one," Pauline grinned, snapping a pass to Amelie.

This time Amelie thought she would try a fake toward the basket and then pull up and shoot. Pauline, however, anticipated the move perfectly. She knocked the ball from Amelie's hands as she brought it up for the shot and took it to the hoop for the game-winning basket, before Amelie even knew what happened.

* * *

At lunch, Amelie's volleyball teammates asked if she was feeling better, seemingly satisfied that her excuse for missing the championship match on Saturday had been legitimate.

I wonder if they would feel any different if they hadn't won, Amelie thought guiltily.

But her friends were still basking in the glory of their victory and were already talking about basketball tryouts, which were starting the following Monday.

"Hey, Jilly," Amelie said when the team hero arrived at the lunch table. "Congratulations! I heard you were totally awesome on Saturday. Way to go!"

"Thanks, Ammi," Jill replied, blushing happily. "I knew that without you and Daria there, I was going to have to come through, but I didn't expect to play *that* well. Of course it helped that everyone else," she indicated her teammates with a gesture, "played great too." She looked back at Amelie. "How *are* you anyway? We were really worried about you."

"Oh, I'm fine," Amelie murmured, feeling wholly undeserving of anyone's sympathy.

"You're going out for basketball, aren't you, Ammi?" Jill asked, changing the subject.

"She'd better be," Daphne piped in. "Did you see her beat Pauline for the first basket in one-on-one?"

"No!" said Mei-lin. "Pauline? Nobody beats Pauline!"

"Well, I didn't beat her," Amelie was quick to admit. "I just got lucky on one move. She's amazing!"

"Yeah, I think she'll be an awesome coach," Daphne added enthusiastically. "She's so much fun. Not that Ms. Bradford isn't, you know. The grade eights are really happy Ms. B. is only coaching them."

"Well, I'm glad we've got Pauline," said Mei-lin. "She's closer to our age. She understands what it's like to be a teenager."

"I think she'll be tough," Quyen suggested. "Tougher than Ms. Bradford. Pauline is really competitive."

The girls nodded their agreement.

"Well, I've got to go for math help," Amelie said wearily, gathering her things. "See you later."

* * *

After a week of morning basketball with Pauline and lunches divided between her friends and math help, the trauma of Amelie's run-in with Anna Archer began to fade.

When she met her friends at lunch on Friday, Amelie proudly waved her retest, which had already been marked with a big 76 percent at the top.

"Excellent!" "Super!" and "Way to go, Ammi!" her friends enthused.

"Come on, Ammi, eat your lunch," Daphne urged. "We've got the first part of the basketball officials' clinic starting in less than ten minutes."

"Jeez, I forgot all about that!" Amelie cried, scrambling to sit down and fish out her lunch at the same time. This was something she had looked forward to since the day Quyen had explained to her how the house league officiating worked. She grinned at her friends and bit into her peanut butter, jelly and potato chip sandwich.

Heading home on the bus that afternoon, Amelie felt a deep sense of satisfaction as she looked back at her week.

Let's see, she thought, counting on her fingers, my foul-shooting has improved to 20 percent. Not exactly WNBA material, but getting there.

Amelie touched the next finger. Fractions, she crowed to herself, I've finally conquered them! She'd felt so relieved when her math teacher had said, "Well, Amelie, if you do fairly well on the probability unit, your March mark should be quite respectable."

And the basketball refereeing clinic had been so much fun. She loved the prospect of being in charge of a game.

Finally, the weekend was looking great, too. On Saturday, Amelie, Jill and Daphne were going to a movie in the early afternoon. Then they would meet Quyen and Mei-lin, who had a Chinese school exam, for ice cream and a little shopping at the Rideau Centre.

Yes, thought Amelie, as she got off the bus at the stop near her house, except for my messed-up family, things are looking up.

13

Basketball Camp

The next few weeks flew by as blizzardy February became blustery March. There was still snow on the ground, but Amelie and her friends could feel spring in the air.

Plans were made for March Break. Daphne was the luckiest of the group in Amelie's eyes. She and her father were spending the entire holiday exploring the rainforest and relaxing on the beaches of Costa Rica. Quyen was traveling with her parents and younger sister, Ming, to Montreal, where Quyen's grandparents and other relatives lived. Mei-lin had to stay home and look after her younger brother while her parents worked. Amelie and Jill were going to the Shooting Stars March Break Basketball Camp.

"Aren't you getting enough basketball?" her mother asked when Amelie had brought up the subject of going to the basketball camp.

"Never!" Amelie answered truthfully. "And it's only in the mornings so I can rest and study and um … do lots of housework," she added slyly.

"Seriously, Ammi, I know you love the game," her mother persisted, "but you're practising five times a week at school and playing at least one game every week. Not to mention the times you and your friends go to the Y to play. I would think you'd have had enough!"

"I know I'm playing a lot, Mom," Amelie replied, "and, you know what? I'm happy."

It was true. The nightmares had subsided, the events of the previous fall were mere memories. Painful memories still, but fading ones.

"And that's what's most important, honey," Marielle Blair responded, hugging her daughter. "I've got to admit, I was certainly impressed with the game I saw your team play last week. You've really improved."

"Thanks, Mom, but I'm still only averaging three for ten on my foul shots. I wish the snow would hurry up and melt and the weather would warm up so I could practise in the driveway."

"I noticed that you don't get fouled as often as the guards do," Marielle observed. She had played high-school basketball herself and Amelie was pleased that her mother was knowledgeable and enthusiastic about the game. "You only went to the line once in that game against Broadbent. Maybe it's hard for you to improve that particular skill because you don't get much chance to do it in a game situation."

Amelie considered her mother's theory. "Hmm … maybe. But for now I think it's a good thing I don't shoot too many free throws. Not until I can make at least six out of ten."

"Well, in that case, I guess we'd better sign you up for that camp!" her mother had said with a smile.

* * *

As March Break grew nearer, so did report cards, Amelie's first from McClung. She was still a little worried about her math and science marks but thought she was doing all right in the rest of the subjects.

Reports were given out on the Friday before school closed down for the break. Amelie met up with Quyen at her second-floor locker. Daphne had already left on her holiday that morning.

"Hey, Ammi," Quyen greeted her friend with a smile. "How's your report card? Are you going to need refuge or anything like that?"

Amelie laughed. "Nah. My parents have never been very high pressure about marks. They know I work pretty hard and I usually do okay." She pulled the report out of its envelope and reviewed it again.

"Wow! I never heard of parents who weren't high pressure about marks," Quyen responded with genuine surprise. "My parents freak out if I get a B!"

"Holy Smokes! My whole report card is Bs and Cs," Amelie admitted. Then, lowering her voice she added, "I even got a D+ in science. It's the first D I've ever had."

"And you won't get in trouble?" Quyen asked wondrously.

"Gosh, Quyen, I don't think so," Amelie replied, unable to relate to her friend's concern. "What about you? Did you get any Bs?"

Quyen looked down briefly, then replied, "Yeah, two actually. One in music and one in design and tech."

"And your parents will be mad?"

"They'll hate it," Quyen answered. Then she grinned when she saw the concern on Amelie's face. "Don't worry, they won't get too upset. The Bs aren't in what they consider important subjects."

"Whew!" Amelie said dramatically, drawing her hand across her brow for effect and completing the gesture with a grin. But the relief she was displaying was not so much for Quyen as it was for herself. With everything else she'd had to deal with in the past several months, Amelie didn't want to worry about her closest friend getting into trouble over two Bs.

* * *

On the Monday morning of March Break, Amelie's mother dropped her off at Ashwood Academy, a private school located in the most affluent part of the city. One of the head coaches for the Shooting Stars basketball club taught physical education at Ashwood and ran a basketball skills camp for girls in grades six, seven and eight.

"Ammi, over here!"

Amelie had just entered the gym, when she heard the familiar voice. Jill was waving at her from the far end of the court. She waved back and dumped her coat and boots in the nearby bleachers before jogging with her gym bag over to where Jill was doing wall stretches.

"Hey, Jilly," Amelie said, greeting her friend with a smile as she laced up her shoes, then joined in the warm-up. "Isn't it great to be here in the gym of the great Coach Andrews?"

"What's so great about him?" Jill asked.

"Don't you remember?" Amelie replied. "Pauline told us he was chosen to coach the provincial boys' team this summer and my brother read in the paper that Coach Andrews expects his team to win the national championship!"

"Well, of course he's going to say that!" Jill laughed. "What do you think, he'll predict that they're going to be big losers?"

"You're right," Amelie conceded. "But, anyway, he's supposed to be an awesome coach."

"Better than Pauline?" Jill asked in mock horror.

The two girls looked at each other for a moment. "Nah," they said together, shaking their heads and laughing. They each took a ball from the cart and started shooting as the gym began to fill up with excited players.

As it turned out, Coach Andrews *was* a good coach and Amelie learned more than she ever thought possible in just one week.

At camp, the participants learned defensive tactics, screening techniques, set plays, presses and press breaks. They dribbled, passed, set screens and trapped. They shot lay-ups, three pointers, jump shots, hook shots and free throws, also known as foul shots, not Amelie's personal favourite.

On the last day of the camp, the coaches organized games and contests. Amelie managed to avoid participating in the foul-shooting competition, although by the end of the week, she was averaging four shots out of ten.

Amelie would be taking part in the speed lay-up drill. She was definitely one of the fastest girls at the camp and had been thrilled when Coach Andrews had praised her agility at combining speed with successful lay-ups from both right and left.

After the first round, Amelie had scored twelve baskets in one minute and she advanced to a second round. This time Amelie and one of the other contestants, a grade-six girl named Mikayla, both scored fourteen baskets, which made them the finalists in the competition.

"You look wiped!" Jill said as she handed Amelie her water bottle.

Amelie could only nod. Her heart was still racing from the fast-paced drill.

"Relax," Jill continued. "You get a fifteen-minute break while we do the foul-shooting contest."

"Good luck, Jilly," Amelie managed at last. She watched as her friend sunk eight out of her ten foul shots and collected the second-place prize in the contest. The winner had made every shot.

Some day, Amelie promised herself, *I'm* going to be able to shoot from the foul line like that, too.

Finally, Amelie and Mikayla each took their positions at a basket for the "shoot-out." Amelie knew she'd probably have to make every shot to win the contest so she concentrated hard on each movement, falling quickly into a rapid-fire rhythm. Just as Amelie thought her lungs would burst and she couldn't lift one more basketball, let alone shoot it, the whistle blew, signaling the end of the minute.

"Yay, Ammi, you made fifteen!" Jill yelled, arriving just in time to support Amelie as her knees buckled from fatigue.

"We have co-winners!" Coach Andrews announced. "Amelie and Mikayla both scored fifteen baskets. Congratulations, girls!" he said, coming to shake Amelie's hand and present her with a laminated basketball poster.

Amelie found Mikayla and shook her hand too. The younger girl was almost as tall as Amelie. "Are you really in grade six?"

Mikayla nodded her head shyly.

"Well, that's pretty amazing. Congratulations," Amelie said sincerely.

"Thanks," Mikayla murmured. "You too."

Amelie decided it was a perfect ending to the week. She realized that she was actually looking forward to getting back to school the next week … and to her team.

14

Getting Ready

Pauline was clearly delighted with the progress Amelie and Jill had made, and she asked them to show her some of the drills they had learned at the camp. The tournament would start in two and a half weeks, and Pauline thought that was enough time to incorporate one or two of the girls' new plays into the Cougars' offence.

On the first day back at school, the team gathered for an early-morning practice. Since the rest of the girls were rusty, they spent most of the practice on conditioning and fundamentals, finishing with a review of the team's offence.

Daphne had returned from Costa Rica with her fair skin lightly tanned. She was full of new experiences she couldn't wait to share with her friends.

"Sorry to interrupt you, Daphne," Pauline said sarcastically, but with a faint hint of a smile. "Let me know when I can carry on with coaching the team."

"Oh, sorry, Coach," Daphne responded sheepishly, clapping a hand over her mouth.

"We're all anxious to hear your tales from the tropics, Daph," the young coach added, "but at the moment, I'd appreciate it if you'd pay attention while I explain what you'll be doing with this little round object called a basketball."

Everyone, including Daphne, giggled and Pauline proceeded to explain the offence, which had all players being in motion most of the time. The guards would bring the ball up the court and pass to one of the forwards on the wing. The guard who made the pass would then cut to the basket in an arcing path toward the ball first, hopefully to get a return pass and then score. It was a simple give-and-go play and the Cougars had used it successfully in their previous games. However, once the opposing team got beat with that play a few times, they could easily have a player get in the way of the return pass and prevent the basket.

So they needed to have several alternate plays once the ball crossed into the front court. It was usually the point guard's responsibility to decide what play would be used, so Daphne's full attention was not only expected, but required. She and Mei-lin, who was designated as the second point guard, were the key players in initiating scoring. Although she hesitated to say anything, Amelie thought the Cougars' point guards were the weakest part of their game.

Daphne was a reasonably good ball handler, that is she could bring the ball up the court well, but her passes were weak and too often intercepted. Mei-lin lacked the aggressiveness of a strong point guard. Most of the Cougars' baskets were scored off of fast breaks, where the defensive rebound would be fired to a player "breaking" to the basket and then going in for the easy lay-up.

With the confidence gained during her week of basketball camp, Amelie finally decided to speak up. She waited until the team had done their cheer and been dismissed to the change room, before approaching Pauline.

"Hey, Coach," Amelie began.

"Hey, yourself, Ammi. What's up?" Pauline responded with a smile as she rolled the ball cart into the equipment room.

"I was just thinking about something Coach Andrews said last week and I thought you might be interested."

"Sure, what is it?" Pauline asked, closing and locking the door.

Amelie suddenly felt awkward. Who was she to make suggestions to someone who knew as much about basketball as Pauline did?

"Well?" Pauline was looking at her now, waiting for an answer.

"Uh ... he said that young coaches usually looked at their smallest players to be guards. That's normal, he said, because they're often the faster, more coordinated players." Amelie took a breath and carried on. "But the *point* guard is such an important position that Coach Andrews says that size should have nothing to do with it. She should be your most athletic, highly skilled player."

"Such as yourself?" Pauline asked.

"No! No, not me," Amelie rushed to explain, embarrassed at the assumption. "I don't have the ball-handling skills. I ... I was thinking of Quyen."

"Quyen? Hmm ..." Pauline pondered that suggestion for a moment, then spoke as if she were talking to herself. "Quyen's got good speed, excellent skills, maybe the best on the team. Most important, she's smart and doesn't panic."

Pauline looked at Amelie. The first bell rang. "I'll give it some thought, Ammi. You've got a point, we *do* need to do something about our offence. A good defensive team will adjust to our fast break in no time. As Amelie turned to leave the gym, Pauline added, "Thanks, Captain."

"Captain?" Amelie responded in surprise, turning back toward her coach.

"You've earned it," Pauline replied, smiling, "by putting in the extra time. You and Jill."

* * *

Amelie admired the way Pauline introduced the change. At their after-school practice on Tuesday, she sat the team down and asked everyone to give their observations on what they thought the strengths and weaknesses of the team were. Some of the girls were unable to specify exactly how the team could be better, but Amelie thought that others were perceptive.

"I've gotta say that, you know, the ball doesn't often make it into the post," Jill offered hesitantly.

"Yeah, and it seems like we commit a lot of turnovers," another girl added.

"I feel like maybe we — the guards, that is — don't take enough outside shots," Mei-lin said quietly.

Then Daphne, who ordinarily displayed supreme confidence in almost any situation, spoke up. "I really like the position of point guard," she began. "Don't get me wrong, it's a lot of fun. But it's scary, too. I haven't played that much basketball before and, to tell you the truth, I'm really not very comfortable in the position."

Everyone looked at her for a surprised moment before Mei-lin added in her quiet voice, "Yeah, Daph and I were talking about how hard it is against some of the stronger teams, to concentrate on protecting the ball, think about the play, and make a good pass to get the offence in motion. We feel like we keep letting the team down."

The team promptly responded, "No way!"

"That's not true."

"You guys are doing a great job!"

Daphne smiled at the support and patted Mei-lin on the shoulder. "Look, I don't want to give it up. I like it and I know I can get better at it with practice. I'm just saying that when you look at what we're trying to do on offence, we need someone really strong at the point to get things going. Mei says she would prefer to be a shooting guard, so if I become the second point, it leaves the starting position open. "

Everyone was quiet. Finally Pauline looked at Amelie. "Ammi, Jill, you're the captains. If we follow Daphne's suggestion, how would you fill the positions?"

Amelie looked at Jill, who shrugged.

"Well," Amelie began, "first of all, I'd like to say that Daphne and Mei have done an amazing job when you consider that they've only started playing basketball two months ago."

A cheer of agreement went up from the team.

"It seems to me that Quyen can practically dribble with her eyes closed," she continued, then stumbled for a moment, remembering how Quyen disliked public praise. "Sorry, Quyen, but it's true. And your passes are always hard and fast and right on target." Amelie looked around at her teammates then brought her gaze back to Pauline. "I think our team will be stronger with Quyen at point guard and then Lucy could move into one of the forward positions. She's already been rebounding more than most guards do."

"How would you feel about trying a change, Lucy? Quyen?" Pauline asked.

Lucy readily agreed that she would rather play closer to the basket than on the perimeter.

Everyone looked at Quyen, who seemed to be thinking. Finally, she spoke, keeping her response typically brief. "I don't want to take away anyone's position," she said. "But if it's available, I'd like to try point guard."

Pauline jumped up from her bench then. "All right then, ladies, let's move it! We've got a game Thursday against Hopevale so we'd better give this new line-up a try!"

Amelie was amazed at how that had worked. Of course, it could have been a disaster. Daphne and Mei-lin had made it easy and Amelie was impressed by the way they'd put the team ahead of themselves.

As it turned out, she was even more impressed at the difference the changes made in the team's performance. Three weeks earlier, the Cougars had beaten Hopevale by one basket, two points. This time, the margin was sixteen.

* * *

The team continued to improve throughout the two weeks leading up to the Eastern Ontario Championships and they were eager to take on teams that they hadn't played before. Schools were coming from as far away as Hawkesbury and Cornwall to the east, Kingston and Belleville to the south and west, and Pembroke and Renfrew from up the Ottawa Valley.

Most of the attention would be focused on the double "A" teams, which was the division the McClung grade-eight team would play in. Many girls on those teams were also players on elite, highly competitive club teams and Amelie looked forward to watching as many games as she could.

The tournament arrived at last and Amelie could see that it was all Pauline could do to keep her players from burning out from all the excitement. As a captain, Amelie did her best to keep her teammates focused, but her own level of enthusiasm was hard enough to control, without taking responsibility for everyone else's.

The Cougars would play two games in their preliminary pool on Wednesday, which was the opening evening of the tournament, and one on Friday. The results of those games would determine their standings in the playoff rounds on Saturday and Sunday.

"Amelie, do you have minute?" It was Ms. Bradford, catching her at the beginning of the lunch hour on Monday. It was a beautiful early spring day, with just a touch of snow still remaining. Amelie was meeting her friends at the chip wagon on Bank Street.

"Sure, Ms. B.," she responded courteously. Her friends would wait for her.

"Come on in," the teacher said, indicating her office door. Amelie followed her and sat down in a chair across from Ms. Bradford's desk.

"Pauline tells me the team is looking good. Are you having fun?"

Amelie nodded enthusiastically. "We're having a blast. Will you be able to watch any of our games?"

"Absolutely, whenever my team isn't playing," Ms. Bradford replied. "I don't want to keep you, Amelie, but I thought I should let you know that Queen Victoria has entered a team in the tournament."

Amelie was quiet for a moment, considering this information, before responding. "I figured they would. Are they in our pool?"

"No," Ms. Bradford answered. "I've tried to place all the Ottawa area teams in pools with schools from out of town. Queen Vic's preliminary pool will be played at Elgin Collegiate. They won't even be at McClung unless they make the playoffs. That's when you could meet up." She paused to let that information sink in. "Now, there are sixteen teams in the division and eight will advance, so the chances of McClung and Queen Vic playing are not ..."

"It's okay, Ms. Bradford," Amelie interrupted quietly.

"Pardon me?"

"I mean, I have a feeling we *will* meet up, but I think I can handle it," Amelie explained.

Ms. Bradford looked at her for a moment. "Amelie, I haven't told anyone about what happened. Pauline doesn't know. Do you think ..." she trailed off.

Amelie had never heard Ms. Bradford run out of words and she wanted to reassure her. "Ms. B., you've been awfully understanding about all this. I know I let you down before, but that's not going to happen again. Pauline doesn't need to know. I'll be fine." Amelie hoped she sounded more confident than she felt. She knew a meeting with her former friends was inevitable. And she desperately hoped she'd be ready for it.

15

The Championships

On Wednesday, Amelie found herself watching the clock all day which, she realized, only made it move more slowly. The Cougars' first game was at 5:00 against a team from Pleasant Corners, near Hawkesbury.

After changing into their uniforms and "warm-ups," Amelie, Quyen, Daphne and Jill went to the gym to watch the 3:30 game between Hopevale and a team from Kingston. They cheered on the hometown school, which was normally their rival, but the girls from Kingston dominated the game from the outset and were leading Hopevale in the final quarter by a score of 42 to 28 when the four friends left for a team meeting with Pauline in the lunchroom.

"Holy Smokes, that Kingston team was strong!" Daphne exclaimed. "Their post player must be close to six feet tall."

"Not quite, Daph," said Amelie indulgently. She had gotten used to Daphne's exaggerations. "She's maybe two inches taller than me and I'm five-seven-and-a-half."

"Well, she looks huge!" Daphne replied.

"Yeah, but she can't jump that well," Quyen observed. "Ammi and Jill can both out-jump her."

"That's true," Daphne conceded as they settled around one of the lunch tables. Everyone else, including Pauline, arrived within a few minutes.

"Well, Cougars," Pauline began her pre-game pep talk, "this is the day we've been working toward for more than eight weeks. How's everybody feeling?"

A chorus of responses erupted.

"Nervous!"

"Excited!"

"Scared!"

"Pumped!"

"Good," Pauline said. "Those are all feelings we should be having. But ..." She let the word hang in the air for a moment, while she waited for everyone's attention. "But we have to take all those feelings and channel them into one big, focused power source."

Amelie quickly glanced around the table at her teammates and saw that, like herself, everyone was trying to concentrate on Pauline's message to them. She knew that focus was the key for this team. They were lacking in the kind of height some of the other teams had. But they had great speed and, when they were on their game, they played together like a finely tuned machine.

Pauline reviewed a few key elements of their game plan and then told them to go to the gym and start warming up. Inside the gym, the noise was deafening. It seemed that every McClung student was in attendance and determined to win the game by sheer force of cheering. Jill set up the tape deck at their basket and, to a high-energy rap, the girls went through a routine that included running, stretching and drills that would warm up all their passing, dribbling and shooting skills.

Afterwards, Pauline huddled with the team and announced the five starting players. "Quyen at point guard, Mei-lin at shooting guard, Layla and Tara at the forward positions, and, Ammi, you're playing post, as usual, and taking the jump ball."

"One — two — three ..." Pauline shouted.

"COUGARS!" the girls yelled in unison.

The bench was screaming their support as the five Cougars took their positions at the centre circle. Amelie's opponent was about the same height as Amelie but, when the ball was tossed up, she was no match for Amelie's jumping ability. The ball was easily tapped ahead to Tara. She grabbed it, pivoted and passed it down the court to Quyen, who was already halfway to the basket with no defensive player near her. She easily caught the perfectly thrown lob, stepped in for a lay-up and scored the first two points of the game.

The spectators erupted but the players did not celebrate. Instead, they immediately set up a pressing defense and forced the opponent throwing the ball in to make a bad pass, which was intercepted by Mei-lin, who shot and scored from the base line. After four minutes of play, the Cougars were up by a score of 12-0 and substitutions were made by both teams. The second group of Cougars on the floor held their own and the first quarter ended with the Cougars ahead 18-6.

Amelie was out again to start the second quarter. Her team took off the press and played half-court defence for the rest of the game. Her teammates were able to get the ball in to Amelie or Jill in the post a number of times and Amelie finished the game, which they won 50-26, with sixteen points and seven rebounds.

"Great game, everyone!" Amelie praised her teammates in the post-game huddle.

"Well done, girls," Pauline said, beaming. "I'm very proud of you. After we shake hands, let's meet for a minute in the lunchroom. Then everybody should grab a bite to eat. Our next game is at eight."

The second game was more challenging. Probably, Amelie thought, because it was late in the evening of a long day. By the time the buzzer sounded to end the game, it was almost

9:30 and the team was almost too exhausted to celebrate their victory with a traditional cheer.

"Ready to go, Sport?" Peter Blair asked, approaching his daughter as she broke from a brief team meeting with Pauline.

Amelie wrapped her arms around her father in a bear hug. "Well, what did you think?" she asked him with a weary smile.

"That was a fine game, Ammi. Maybe not quite as energetic as the earlier one, but you girls certainly got the job done!"

"Yeah," Amelie agreed. "I'm beat. It's a good thing we're not playing tomorrow. I don't think I'd last five minutes."

"In that case," Amelie's father said with a wink, "we'd better get you home to bed right away and forget about the Dairy Bar stop for a double Chocolate Avalanche."

"Oh, Daddy," Amelie replied, laughing, "you know I'm never too tired for ice cream!"

* * *

The final game in their pool was at 5:00 on Friday and the Cougars were being challenged by a team from Russell, a small town outside of Ottawa. The game was tied at the end of regulation time and an extra four-minute period had to be played.

The Russell team had a big, strong girl in the post whose play demonstrated her experience and confidence. Whenever one of the wings managed to make a successful pass to Amelie, the opponent would anticipate her move and expertly slide into just the right position to prevent Amelie from scoring. When Amelie was able to get a shot away, she was either off-balance or shooting blind and, not only did she miss many of her shots, but the opposing player was in position to block her out and grab the rebound, setting up a scoring opportunity for her team.

Amelie had been mildly frustrated throughout the game by her inability to outmaneuver the girl she was up against but, fortunately, Mei-lin was sinking everything she shot and several other Cougars scored personal bests to keep the team in the game. Nevertheless, in the closing moments of the overtime period, McClung was down 32-30 with ten seconds left in the game. Amelie was in the mid-post position and trying to signal Quyen to use her as a screen and take the ball to the basket.

To Amelie's surprise and dismay, Quyen misunderstood and fired the ball to her. With only a few seconds remaining, Amelie had no choice but to shoot. She faked with her body toward the base line and was thrilled to sense her defensive player start to move in that direction. Amelie quickly pivoted to go through the key instead, but the player guarding her recovered from her initial mistake and moved directly into Amelie's path just as she was releasing the ball toward the hoop.

As Amelie bounced hard off her sturdy opponent and watched the ball hit the backboard without dropping through the net, she heard the referee's whistle blow and assumed that the game had ended and that the Cougars had lost. But she was wrong.

"Number eleven, you're shooting two," the referee was saying to Amelie, while supervising the lining up of the teams for the free throws.

They'd called her opponent for a blocking foul, Amelie realized wondrously. Oh no, she thought, not me, not foul shots.

She took her place on the free-throw line and shot a worried glance at Pauline on the bench. Quyen gave her a pat on the shoulder, then went to her own position on the side of the key. Amelie looked at the clock.

Three seconds, she thought. She knew the clock wouldn't start during her first shot. The time would only begin if she missed the second shot or, if she made it, the clock would start as soon as the ball was thrown in by the opponent and touched by any player. Either way, unless she made both foul shots to tie the game, the Cougars would end up second in their pool and have to meet a first-place team in the first round of the playoffs. Her foul-shooting percentage had risen to five out of ten, 50 percent. What she needed here, Amelie thought desperately, was nothing less than a 100 percent.

The gym was quiet. Amelie focused her attention on her form, setting her feet just so on the foul line, bending her knees and sticking her bottom out behind. She bounced the ball twice and twirled it in her hands to get it set in just the right position. She peered at the back of the rim over the ball, flexed her knees, took a deep breath and, straightening her legs, flipped the ball off her fingertips with a little backspin. The ball looped in a lovely rainbow arc directly into the net. Swish!

A cheer went up from the bench and the spectators as the Cougars moved to within one point of a tie and the chance to play another overtime period. Her teammates on the floor stepped forward to give Amelie quick high-fives as she waited for the referee to hand her the ball for the second shot.

"Relax," Quyen whispered, "it's not the Olympics."

Amelie set herself up again for the shot. She felt as though she were performing the identical action she had just completed successfully but, as the ball rolled from her fingers, she knew immediately that it was ever so-slightly misdirected. It would hit the rim but it wasn't going to drop.

The opposing team had the same realization, but they also made a fatal mistake: they forgot about the three seconds and started to celebrate. As they grabbed one another for joyous victory hugs, Quyen stepped toward the basket and jumped up to rebound Amelie's misguided shot. While still unbalanced in the air, she released the ball softly against the backboard. The sudden stunned silence on the court and from the spectator benches was broken by the honking sound of the buzzer ending the game. Every eye in the gym watched as Quyen fell awkwardly to the floor, while the basketball fell silently through the net.

Amelie's despair from her missed shot turned to elation as she realized that the Cougars had won the game. She ran over to Quyen, who was still lying on the floor, a pained expression on her face.

"Quyen! Are you hurt?" Amelie asked, taking her friend's hand in her own.

"It's my ankle. I rolled over on it when I came down," Quyen responded, grimacing.

"Let's have a look at it." Ms. Bradford, who had been watching the game from the sidelines, was kneeling at Quyen's feet and gently probing the injured ankle. "You girls go ahead and shake hands. The other team is waiting," she instructed Amelie and her teammates.

While the two teams went by each other, shaking hands and saying "Good game," Ms. Bradford helped Quyen up and supported her as she hopped to the bench on her good foot to the cheers of everyone in the gym.

Minutes later, Amelie and other members of the team carried Quyen across the hall to the lunchroom where an ice pack was quickly applied. Quyen's parents were called to come pick her up and were told that she might need an X-ray.

"Well, Quyen, you were certainly thinking in *that* game. That was an incredible play you made," Pauline said with enthusiasm.

Amelie was about to add her agreement when Quyen spoke up in a strong voice. "Wait a minute," she began. "I made a lucky shot. But it was Ammi who made the decision to miss the second foul shot so we could have the chance to win, instead of just tie."

Amelie stared dumbly at Quyen. Pauline was also looking at Quyen, but then turned her attention to Amelie.

"Quyen's right, you know," Pauline said thoughtfully. "We would have had a tough time playing double overtime. You girls were tired. A tie wasn't good enough; we needed the win. Good thinking, Ammi."

"But …" Amelie started to explain that she hadn't meant to miss the second shot.

"Yeah," Quyen interrupted as her gaze met Amelie's. "Maybe you didn't even realize it, Ammi, but if making that shot would have won the game for us, you'd have made it."

"But …" Amelie tried again.

"I think that's true, Amelie," Pauline said, breaking eye contact with Quyen. "You did exactly what we needed. I should have called a time-out and *told* you to miss the second shot. I'll certainly remember that in the future." She paused for a moment. "And it was a good thing Quyen understood the play and followed through."

"Gosh, Quyen," Amelie said, reminded of her friend's injury. "I sure hope your ankle is okay."

"Don't worry," Quyen replied, smiling weakly. "It was worth it."

Quyen's parents entered the lunchroom and Amelie and Pauline supported the injured girl around the shoulders as she hobbled out to the yard where the car was waiting.

As Amelie held on to her friend and helped her slide into the back seat, propping Quyen's injured leg up, she said quietly, "Thanks for making me look good, Quyen."

Quyen then whispered something in Amelie's ear and the two girls squeezed each other's hand before Amelie softly closed the car door.

Amelie watched as the car pulled away. She hugged herself in the coolness of the early spring evening. Quyen had demonstrated her loyalty as a friend by saying that Amelie's miss had been intentional. But Quyen's whispered message had emphasized the faith she had in Amelie and expected Amelie to have in herself. Amelie knew that this was a friendship that would not be easily destroyed.

"You didn't need me or anybody else to make you look good. You *are* good," Quyen had whispered. "And when you need to, trust me, you'll be awesome."

16

On the Line

Amelie's father and her brother, Luke, watched the dramatic Friday game and the three of them went out for fast food afterwards.

"Smart thinking, Sport," Peter Blair said to Amelie after they'd gotten settled in the Land Rover. "Not many young players would have thought to miss that second foul shot without the coach telling them to."

"Duh, she didn't miss it on purpose," Luke said. Amelie's brother was never shy about contributing his opinion.

"Luke's right," Amelie admitted. "I'm just a 50 percent free-throw shooter, Dad. We were lucky Quyen was paying attention."

"If you'd just do what I taught you last summer, Ammi, you'd get that 50 percent up," Luke insisted. "The shots you make are perfect. But you're not focusing on *every* shot. You're not putting your hand in the basket on *every* shot."

"Well, regardless of what was intended, the game ended well," Peter Blair said as he pulled up to the restaurant's drive-through window. "But your brother's absolutely right, Amelie. You're not a 50 percent shooter, you're a 100 percent shooter who is concentrating on only 50 percent of your shots," he concluded.

* * *

The quarter and semifinal games were scheduled on Saturday and the finals, if the Cougars got that far, would be played on Sunday. Amelie had checked the boards before leaving the tournament and noticed that Queen Victoria had come second in their pool and would be facing the big, tough team from Kingston in a quarterfinal game Saturday morning. Amelie was relieved when she realized that the Queen Vic Royals were likely to get their clocks cleaned by the outstanding Kingston squad. The McClung Cougars would face a team from Cornwall in their quarterfinal match at 8:00 Saturday morning.

Peter Blair dropped Luke off at home after supper but Amelie was staying with her father, who was more than happy to get up with her and drive to the school for the early game. Amelie had a little trouble getting to sleep, thinking about Quyen and whether she would be all right to play. The team would be considerably weakened without Quyen in the point guard position. But even her concerns for her friend and for her team could not keep Amelie awake for long. She fell into a restless sleep, tossing and turning for an hour or so before her exhausted body gave in and allowed her to rest peacefully until the alarm sounded at 6:00 the next morning.

* * *

The first thing Amelie saw when she entered the gym at 7:20 Saturday morning was Daphne seated on the bench next to Quyen, who wore a cast on her lower leg and had a pair of crutches propped up next to her.

"Oh no!" Amelie cried, running over to where they sat.

"Yeah," Quyen responded wearily. "I was in Emergency at Children's until one o'clock this morning. It's just a sprain. I can't believe they put a cast on a sprain!"

"Well, you must need it," Amelie scolded.

"Isn't this awful?" Jill asked, joining the girls.

Amelie looked at Quyen for a moment. "Awful?" she asked, directing her reply to Jill. "What's so awful? At least we've got Quyen here to cheer us on and Daph's more than ready to step up and do the job. We're in great shape!" Amelie wished she felt as confident as she sounded. But she took her role as team captain seriously and felt she should convey a positive attitude, whatever the situation.

Daphne looked doubtful.

"Hey, Daph, do you realize how much you've improved from the point since you gave up the starting position a couple weeks ago?" Amelie demanded.

"No kidding, Daph," Quyen added, supporting Amelie's pep talk. "You're definitely ready to start. You know the plays inside out and your crossover dribble is good enough now to get you by any defender."

Daphne's pixie face lit up. She seemed bolstered by Amelie and Quyen's support. Even Jill's outlook appeared to have been converted from doom to optimism.

The rest of the team arrived and they began warming up together.

The McClung team had lucked into an easy matchup for their quarterfinal. Even without Quyen, the Cougars never trailed the opponent in the entire game and won by a score of 46-31. Daphne played a solid game, her passes having improved considerably. She even scored two baskets and was three for three from the foul line.

"Hey, seven points is a record for me," Daphne crowed with delight.

In the post-game meeting, Pauline seemed a little tense. "Good game, girls," she began with sincerity. "But from here on, it's going to have to be better than good. If you want those gold medals, you'll have to earn them. Our semifinal will be against the winner of the Kingston-Queen Vic game, which should be getting started," she glanced at the clock on the wall, "… right about now. These are good teams. Let's see what we can pick up from watching them play. "

The team spent several more minutes in conference, then broke up. Most of the girls headed into the canteen line-up to get their sugar fix. Amelie and Quyen returned to the gym to watch Kingston play Queen Victoria.

Amelie could feel Quyen's eyes on her as she watched the game. Jessie was Queen Vic's point guard and her quick feet were making problems for the bigger, but slower, Kingston team.

"She's good," Quyen commented simply.

Amelie didn't reply immediately. Then, "Yeah, she sure is," was all she said.

Amelie's attention had turned to Anna Archer playing in the post position. She was tall and agile and made moves that showed she'd been well coached. She had little trouble out-maneuvering the tall Kingston player Amelie and her friends had admired earlier in the tournament.

Amelie's opinion of the Kingston team did not change. They were big, strong and highly skilled. But they could not out-run the Queen Victoria Royals. Nor could they out-shoot them. Jessie and Anna led their team to a 56-50 win, scoring twenty-two of the Royals' points. The McClung Cougars were not encouraged; it was clear that they would have their work cut out for them. At 4:00 they would play a semifinal against Queen Victoria, who had just defeated a team the girls had thought was possibly the strongest one in their division.

* * *

By the time the McClung-Queen Victoria game arrived, the other semifinal had been decided. The Colonel By Middle School Hornets would be the team to beat in the finals on Sunday and it was no secret that they were confident of winning in the championship game.

While warming up, Amelie tried to get herself focused and to shut out the many distractions in the gym. There was the buzz of spectators, the bouncing of balls as both teams ran through dribbling, passing and shooting drills, and the continuous babble of her own teammates as they tried to psyche each other up during the pre-game routine. As much as she wanted to believe this game didn't matter, Amelie knew that it *did* matter — in ways that had little to do with the score.

She had both feared and imagined this "reunion" with her former friends more times than she cared to remember. Now she was aware of the quickening of her heartbeat, her sweating palms and her tangled emotions.

These girls — Anna Archer, at least — had tried to destroy her. But they had not succeeded. Almost, Amelie thought, but not quite. Jessie, whether intentionally or not, had almost broken her heart. But somehow her spirit had remained strong and Amelie realized in that moment that she was even stronger now for what she had endured. Her family and her new friends had helped her through, but it was her own determination to survive that had prevailed.

The intensity of the competition was apparent from the tip-off. Cougar teammates had heard that members of the Queen Victoria squad who had also played on the volleyball team, were out to avenge their big loss at the McClung tournament in January.

Amelie was up against Anna for the toss of the ball to start the game. Anna's face was set in a mask of intense indifference. She gave no indication that she even knew Amelie, completely avoiding eye contact.

She's trying to make me feel invisible, Amelie thought with surprise. She'd expected something more along the lines of outright hostility and "trash talk."

Well, two can play this ignoring game, Amelie decided. The ball was tossed and despite Anna's height advantage, Amelie out-jumped her to tip the ball to Tara, who pivoted and passed the ball to Daphne on her way to the basket. However, the Royals seemed to have anticipated the Cougars' standard jump-ball play and Jessie was in Daphne's path to the basket. Daphne pulled up and made a jump shot which rolled around the rim three times before dropping through the net.

Amelie's spirits soared as she dropped back to her defensive position for the press. Making her first shot under pressure would, Amelie knew, increase Daphne's confidence. Sure enough, Daphne stole the ball off the Royals' throw-in and passed to Amelie breaking into the key. Anna had set up in her team's offensive end and no defensive player had switched to cover Amelie, who scored on the easy lay-up.

The Royals called a time-out and returned to the game with an effective press break that let them bring the ball across into their front court. Once there, Jessie demonstrated the shooting skill that had won her endless games of driveway twenty-one against Amelie, in what seemed to Amelie to be the very distant past. Daphne was no match for Jessie's quickness and, being even shorter than Jessie, was not an effective shot blocker. Amelie saw the problem and signaled to Pauline to call a time-out.

When the Cougars returned to the floor, Amelie was responsible for guarding Jessie, and Tara, who was the next-tallest player, took over defending Anna. Anticipating the opposing team's adjustment, Jessie ran a new offence and succeeded in getting the ball into Anna in the post. Without Amelie to oppose her, Anna easily moved around Tara for lay-ups.

By the end of the first quarter, it was obvious that Amelie, who was by far the Cougars' best defensive player, could not cover Jessie and Anna at the same time and both girls were big scoring threats. The Cougars were down 8-12.

"Okay, girls," Pauline announced. "Let's go into our zone defence."

Amelie thought this was a good move. Each player would now cover an area of the key rather than a specific opponent. The strategy was effective. Amelie could come out and challenge Jessie when she had the ball, and the zone made it difficult for the Royals to get the ball to Anna inside the key. At halftime, the teams were tied, 18-18. The zone defence made for a low-scoring game but certainly worked more to McClung's advantage than it did to Queen Victoria's.

Amelie was surprised that neither Jessie nor Anna were making any obvious attempts to rattle her. They both seemed to be intensely focused on the game. But Amelie did notice that Anna's frustration seemed to be increasing as the game progressed and she was not getting the scoring opportunities she was undoubtedly used to.

In the halftime huddle, Pauline instructed the team. "The zone has worked well so far to slow them down, girls. You've done a great job." She gave them her broadest smile.

"But," Pauline continued, holding up a cautionary finger, "they're well coached. They will adjust in the second half. Watch for them to make quick passes around the perimeter and wait patiently for an opening in your zone. Stay focused. Keep the pressure on them."

Amelie couldn't resist adding, "Watch number twelve, the post player. She's really frustrated. She's already got three personal fouls, so if you can get the ball in to me, I might be able to draw another foul."

"Careful, Ammi," Quyen said quietly from the bench.

Amelie looked at her and nodded, then surprised herself by saying, "Don't worry, Quyen. I'm not afraid of her."

The intensity of the game heated up in the second half but the lead went back and forth, staying close. Both teams had already played a game earlier in the day and fatigue was setting in. The Cougars were unable to take and keep a lead. They would go up by a basket and the Royals would respond with two.

As the closing minutes of the game approached, McClung was behind 32-36. Amelie watched from the bench, enjoying her last minute of rest before she would go back on to finish the game.

"Remember the Russell game," Quyen whispered to her as Amelie eyed the scoreboard. "The game's not over until that final buzzer sounds."

"But yesterday we had you," Amelie reminded her friend. She glanced at the scoreboard again. Two and a half minutes left.

On the floor, she watched Anna nail Jill on the top of the head as she tried to put up a jump shot.

Whistle. It was Anna's fifth foul; she was out of the game. Amelie could see that Anna was seething and wondered where all that anger came from.

As Amelie continued to watch, Anna turned and said something to the referee who had made the call. Amelie was too far away to hear what was said, but she saw the shock, then anger, on the official's face. She blasted her whistle again and made a "T" with her hands, signaling a technical foul.

The Queen Victoria coach walked out onto the floor, took Anna by the elbow and led her over to the bench. Amelie looked quickly at Jessie to catch her reaction to the scene, but Jessie's eyes were cast down at the floor. Amelie noticed that she was clenching and unclenching her fists. It was a gesture Amelie knew well. Jessie was upset.

Jill missed her first foul shot but made the second and Pauline selected her to take the two technical foul shots as well. She made both, and McClung pulled to within one point of the Royals.

"Okay, Ammi, you're on," Pauline said from behind the bench.

The last substitution of the game was made and Amelie took to the floor, determined to take full advantage of Anna's absence. However, both teams hung tough on defence and the seconds on the clock ticked away with no scoring taking place.

With less than thirty seconds to play, the Royals had possession of the ball and were trying to run out the clock with dribbling and quick passes. In the event that it came down to this very situation, Amelie had been told by Pauline to purposely foul one of the opponents to stop the clock and try to get the ball back by rebounding what they hoped would be missed foul shots. The time had come. As soon as Jessie passed to her shooting guard, Amelie immediately ran into the unsuspecting girl. She softened the impact as best she could and no damage was done.

"Sorry," she murmured.

The whistle blew and the guard went to the free-throw line.

Without Anna in the line-up, Amelie gambled that Tara and Layla could handle the job of rebounding and she dropped back behind the free-throw line, edging toward centre court. She could see Jessie watching her out of the corner of her eye. But, with only four seconds on the clock, a one-point lead, and the possibility of two more points from foul shots, it appeared that Jessie did not take Amelie as a serious threat to their victory.

The first free throw went wide and the McClung crowd cheered the miss. The second shot, however, looked like it was right on the money. The ball, thrown hard, hit the backboard and bounced to the front of the rim where it deflected back up to the top right-hand corner of the glass. Amelie waited just long enough to see Layla launch herself into the air, arms outreached toward the basketball, before she took off down the court.

"LONG!" Amelie cried as she looked over her shoulder at Layla, who was just releasing a baseball pass in her direction. She had a head start of several steps on Jessie, the only close defender. She saw the clock click to three seconds as the ball fell into her outstretched hands. She had to take a dribble to get within shooting range. The clock clicked to two. She picked up her dribble, took two steps and flew into the air, bringing the ball up to shoot.

As she was about to release it, Amelie was pushed violently from behind causing her airborne position to become completely unbalanced. The ball flew wildly out of her hands. She heard both the sound of the referee's whistle and the game-ending buzzer as she crashed to the floor, where she lay struggling to catch the wind that had been knocked out of her when she landed.

"Ammi, Ammi, are you all right?" It was Jessie, kneeling beside her. But Amelie was still gasping for air and couldn't respond.

"I'm so sorry, Ammi. I'm ... I'm sorry for everything," Jessie was saying, but she was gently pulled away by Ms. Bradford, whose look of concern alarmed Amelie.

Finally she was able to draw a deep breath. "I'm okay, Ms. B. Really. I just got the wind knocked out of me."

Pauline was leaning over her now too and Amelie hastened to reassure her coaches by moving and shaking all her limbs. The crowd roared as Ms. Bradford and Pauline helped Amelie to her feet.

She looked over to where her father, mother and brother sat looking worried until she smiled at them and called out, "I'm fine."

"Listen, Cougars," Pauline instructed during the time-out. "We can win this game in an overtime period with their number twelve fouled out of the game."

Amelie and the rest of the team nodded their agreement.

"Okay, Ammi, we all know foul shooting isn't your favourite skill of the game." Pauline gazed at Amelie briefly before continuing. "But you only need to make one of the two shots, 50 percent, to tie the game and put us into overtime. What do you think?"

Amelie merely nodded once, then walked out onto the floor and took her customary position on the free-throw line. She was alone. The game was over, there was no time on the clock, the players were all on the sidelines. While the referee waited for her to be ready, Amelie looked at the Queen Victoria bench and saw that Anna was sitting alone at the end of the bench, smirking at her. Amelie guessed that Anna was well aware of her foul-shooting difficulties.

Jessie sat next to her coach, her eyes red-rimmed and moist. She met Amelie's gaze and offered up a small, humble smile. Amelie returned it. As the referee stepped forward with the ball extended to her, Amelie looked around again to where her family sat. Luke flipped his hand and mouthed the words, "Put your hand in the basket." Peter and Marielle Blair simply smiled and nodded at her.

Amelie understood the importance of this moment. Not because she was in a position to win, lose or tie the game. Not because she had to prove herself in the foul-shooting department. Just as Quyen had said before, Amelie remembered, it's not the Olympics.

She went through her preparations and took the first shot. Hand in the basket, she thought, and her fingers flipped forward and followed the ball right through the net. An explosion of cheers erupted from all over the gym.

No, what was important about this moment was the fact that she had finally faced her fears and they had evaporated. She even felt sorry for Anna, who she now recognized as a big, insecure bully who had succeeded in manipulating Amelie's best friend. It appeared that she was not so successful at doing that anymore.

As she twirled the ball in her hands, preparing for the second shot, Amelie briefly wondered what had happened to Anna to make her so unhappy.

It was time to focus. She didn't need this basket.

But she was going to make it.

Epilogue

The Courage to Forgive

Toward the end of the championship game on Sunday against the Colonel By Hornets, the Cougars were in a time-out huddle with Pauline, when Amelie noticed Jessie enter the gym by herself and take a seat on one of the spectator benches.

Queen Victoria's bronze-medal game against Russell must be over, Amelie thought. She didn't notice a medal around Jessie's neck but that didn't mean anything. She could have put it away already.

"So let's hang in there, girls," Pauline was urging. "Just two and a half minutes to go. You're doing great! One — two — three …"

"COUGARS!" the players cried.

The Cougars held a 43-36 lead against the surprised Hornets. The girls and their young coach had learned a lot during the tournament and they were applying all of it in this game to try and win the championship for their school. Ms. Bradford's grade eights had already been eliminated from their division in a tough quarterfinal.

The Hornets became more unraveled as the seconds slipped away. They were a good team but had struggled with scoring throughout the game. Amelie thought Daphne and Mei-lin had been brilliant in the point guard position. She was so happy that her friends would end the season feeling good about themselves.

Just then Layla passed the ball into her in the low post. Amelie spun toward the base line and laid the ball up against the glass as softly as a whisper. It dropped into the net and the buzzer sounded to end the game.

Amelie jumped up and down with her teammates in jubilation over their victory. The teams shook hands and assembled on the floor for a formal awards presentation of the gold and silver medals. The whole team held hands. Amelie stood between Quyen and Jill and could not help grinning from ear to ear. She looked out at her fractured but loving family among the many McClung fans applauding from the sidelines as the medals were hung around each girl's neck.

When Amelie received hers, she heard, above the whistles and cheers of her family and friends, a familiar voice yelling, "All right, Ammi, way to go!"

She looked toward the sound of the voice and met Jessie's eyes. Amelie felt an understanding pass between them as Jessie moved to the exit with a brief, sad little wave of her hand. They would never again be friends. There had been too much pain, too much had been said and done, too much had been lost.

But there could be forgiveness. And someday they might even be able to talk about what had happened, what had gone wrong.

For now, Amelie had some celebrating to do ... with her friends.

Other books you'll enjoy in the Sports Stories series...

Baseball

☐ *Curve Ball* by John Danakas #1
Tom Poulos is looking forward to a summer of baseball in Toronto until his mother puts him on a plane to Winnipeg.

☐ *Baseball Crazy* by Martyn Godfrey #10
Rob Carter wins an all-expenses-paid chance to be batboy at the Blue Jays' spring training camp in Florida.

☐ *Shark Attack* by Judi Peers #25
The East City Sharks have a good chance of winning the county championship until their arch rivals get a tough new pitcher.

Basketball

☐ *Fast Break* by Michael Coldwell #8
Moving from Toronto to small-town Nova Scotia was rough, but when Jeff makes the school basketball team he thinks things are looking up.

☐ *Camp All-Star* by Michael Coldwell #12
In this insider's view of a basketball camp, Jeff Lang encounters some unexpected challenges.

☐ *Nothing but Net* by Michael Coldwell #18
The Cape Breton Grizzly Bears face an out-of-town basketball tournament they're sure to lose.

☐ *Slam Dunk* by Steven Barwin and Gabriel David Tick #23
In this sequel to *Roller Hockey Blues*, Mason Ashbury's basketball team adjusts to the arrival of some new players: girls.

☐ *Courage on the Line* by Cynthia Bates #33
After Amelie changes schools, she must confront difficult former teammates in an extramural match.

Figure Skating

☐ *A Stroke of Luck* by Kathryn Ellis #6
Strange accidents are stalking one of the skaters at the Millwood Arena.

☐ *The Winning Edge* by Michele Martin Bosley #28
Jennie wants more than anything to win a grueling series of competitions, but is success worth losing her friends?

Gymnastics

☐ *The Perfect Gymnast* by Michele Martin Bossley #9
Abby's new friend has all the confidence she needs, but she also has a serious problem that nobody but Abby seems to know about.

Ice Hockey

☐ *Two Minutes for Roughing* by Joseph Romain #2
As a new player on a tough Toronto hockey team, Les must fight to fit in.

☐ *Hockey Night in Transcona* by John Danakas #7
Cody Powell gets promoted to the Transcona Sharks' first line, bumping out the coach's son who's not happy with the change.

☐ *Face Off* by C.A. Forsyth #13
A talented hockey player finds himself competing with his best friend for a spot on a select team.

☐ *Hat Trick* by Jacqueline Guest #20
The only girl on an all-boys' hockey team works to earn the captain's respect and her mother's approval.

☐ *Hockey Heroes* by John Danakas #22
A left-winger on the thirteen-year-old Transcona Sharks adjusts to a new best friend and his mom's boyfriend.

☐ *Hockey Heat Wave* by C.A. Forsyth #27
In this sequel to *Face Off*, Zack and Mitch encounter some trouble when it looks like only one of them will make the select team at hockey camp.

☐ *Shoot to Score* by Sandra Richmond #31
Playing defence on the B list, alongside the coach's mean-spirited son, are tough obstacles for Steven to overcome, but he perseveres and changes his luck.

Riding

☐ *A Way With Horses* by Peter McPhee #11
A young Alberta rider invited to study show jumping at a posh local riding school uncovers a secret.

☐ *Riding Scared* by Marion Crook #15
A reluctant new rider struggles to overcome her fear of horses.

☐ *Katie's Midnight Ride* by C.A. Forsyth #16
An ambitious barrel racer finds herself without a horse weeks before her biggest rodeo.

☐ *Glory Ride* by Tamara L. Williams #21
Chloe Anderson fights memories of a tragic fall for a place on the Ontario Young Riders' Team.

☐ *Cutting it Close* by Marion Crook #24
In this novel about barrel racing, a talented young rider finds her horse is in trouble just as she is about to compete in an important event.

Roller Hockey

☐ *Roller Hockey Blues* by Steven Barwin and Gabriel David Tick #17
Mason Ashbury faces a summer of boredom until he makes the roller-hockey team.

Running

☐ *Fast Finish* by Bill Swan #30
Noah is a promising young runner headed for the provincial finals when he suddenly decides to withdraw from the event.

Sailing

☐ *Sink or Swim* by William Pasnak #5
Dario can barely manage the dog paddle, but thanks to his mother he's spending the summer at a water sports camp.

Soccer

☐ *Lizzie's Soccer Showdown* by John Danakas #3
When Lizzie asks why the boys and girls can't play together, she finds herself the new captain of the soccer team.

☐ *Alecia's Challenge* by Sandra Diersch #32
Thirteen-year-old Alecia has to cope with a new school, a new stepfather, and friends who have suddenly discovered the opposite sex.

Swimming

☐ *Breathing Not Required* by Michele Martin Bossley #4
An eager synchronized swimmer works hard to be chosen for a solo and almost loses her best friend in the process.

☐ *Water Fight!* by Michele Martin Bossley #14
Josie's perfect sister is driving her crazy but when she takes up swimming — Josie's sport — it's too much to take.

☐ *Taking a Dive* by Michele Martin Bossley #19
Josie holds the provincial record for the butterfly, but in this sequel to *Water Fight,* she can't seem to match her own time and might not go on to the nationals.

☐ *Great Lengths* by Sandra Diersch #26
Fourteen-year-old Jessie decides to find out whether the rumours about a new swimmer at her Vancouver club are true.

Track and Field

☐ *Mikayla's Victory* by Cynthia Bates #29
Mikayla must compete against her friend if she wants to represent her school at an important track event.